"I really liked the second book in the *Zan-Gah* series. It has a great plot line, and a lot of drama."
— Elan S., age 15

"The author has painted a richly colored landscape and filled it with vibrant characters. Themes of forgiveness, dealing with hatred, brains overcoming might, and intense love for another person, add great depth to the story....Great material for high school students."
— Barry Crook, Library Media Specialist

"I was completely caught up in *Zan-Gah: A Prehistoric Adventure,* and have now read the equally gripping sequel, *Zan-Gah and the Beautiful Country.* Once again Shickman has provided a host of richly realized characters, a fabulous sense of place, and lots of action....I found many parallels to today's world, and thought on numerous occasions how this book could lead to great discussions with school groups. But in the end it is the rich characters and believable action that carry the day. *Zan-Gah and the Beautiful Country* should find a ready audience with those who have enjoyed Gary Paulsen's *Hatchet,* Watt Key's *Alabama Moon,* or Michelle Paver's *Wolf Brother.* A most worthy read."
— Joe Corbett, School Librarian

"*Zan-Gah and the Beautiful Country* is an engaging, thought-provoking, and genuinely exciting novel. Allan Shickman has a definite gift for storytelling."
— Kurt S., ESL Instructor

"I had not associated human virtues and failings to the primitive men and women who preceded the present day human race until my reading of *Zan-Gah and the Beautiful Country.*"
—Donald S., Court Administrator

"Once I started reading *Zan-Gah and the Beautiful Country*, I couldn't put it down! I had to see what Dael was going to do next!"
— Donald L., Professor of Mathematics

"Riveting....Young and old alike will enjoy and be moved by this exquisitely written story."
— Gerard S., PhD, Psychology

PRAISE FOR
ZAN-GAH: A PREHISTORIC ADVENTURE:

"Allan Richard Shickman's *Zan-Gah* is a terrifically exciting adventure that will appeal to young adults and their elders too. Richly imagined and beautifully written, with characters and settings unlike any I've read, I believe *Zan-Gah* will be read and reread for many years to come."
— Scott Phillips, Best-Selling Author of *The Ice Harvest* and *Cottonwood*

"Highly recommended for young adult library collections."
— *The Midwest Book Review: Children's Bookwatch*

"*Zan-Gah* is told with such verve, energy, and style that it will appeal to readers of all ages and sensibilities....Shickman's lively imagination is obvious on every page....The power of Shickman's words becomes apparent in the very first chapter....heart-pounding prose..."
— Robert A. Cohn, *St. Louis Jewish Light*

"I refused to turn off the lights because I was enjoying *Zan-Gah* so much, and the next day...I took it with me on the subway to get those last few pages in between Brooklyn and Manhattan. This 35-year-old loved it...I kept saying 'I know it's supposed to be a children's book...but it's really, *really* good!!!'"
— Sadie N., Yoga Master

"*Zan-Gah* is one of the best books I ever read…a truly gripping book. The characters are so real I feel like I know them. I give the book five stars. I could read it over and over."
— Sam L., age 13

"We have given this book to all four grandchildren, ages 11, 14, 18, 22. Each of them loved it.…My husband and I are in our 60s—we loved it, too."
— Lou M., Grandparent

"I liked *Zan-Gah* so much that I bought a copy for every student in the class."
— Rosalie B., Teacher and Volunteer

"We love *Zan-Gah* at S. Middle School. It is always checked out of the library."
— Pat L., Library Media Specialist

"My mom is always on me for not reading.…But I think I've found a perfect book for me, and that book is *Zan-Gah*."
— Marissa B., age 11

"I always recommend books the entire family could read and discuss. *Zan-Gah* is the perfect book for boys, girls, teens, parents, and grandparents.…You will love it!"
— Joan B., Middle and High School
Reading Teacher

"I am a nurse practitioner and my brain is always in diagnostic mode. Dael definitely has post-traumatic stress disorder and maybe a smidge of bipolar disorder. Interesting reading, in fact I think I'll read it again."
— Johnette R., Nurse

"It is refreshing to see a book of this quality published for pre-teens and teens. It is age appropriate in content, but still challenges the intellect of avid readers of this age group. I know several kids who will want to read *Zan-Gah*."
— Diane P., Editor

FOR MY WIFE

ZAN-GAH

AND THE BEAUTIFUL COUNTRY

By Allan Richard Shickman

EARTHSHAKER BOOKS

ZAN-GAH: And the Beautiful Country

ISBN: 978-0-9790357-1-5
LCCN: 2009924462

Published in the United States by
Earthshaker Books
P. O. Box 300184
St. Louis, MO 63130

VISIT OUR WEBSITE AT **WWW.ZAN-GAH.COM**

CONTENTS

1 "IT IS TIME"

When Lissa-Na died, Dael wept real tears. No one blamed him—except for Dael himself, who was shocked at his own melting. Through his long, nightmarish captivity, suffering humiliation and torture at the hands of enemy peoples, he had never shed a drop. They had afflicted him in every way they could invent, both physically and mentally, for fully two years, but Dael never allowed tears to fall from his eyes—although he had been no more than a gentle, dreamy child at the time he was captured. Savage strangers had held this boy in a tiny cage and used him with whatever cruelty they could invent. It had been their sport! (No one who knows his gods should speak of these things.) But if they had hoped to break his spirit they failed. Dael stored his tears and gave his enemies no reward. Hidden within his softness was a staff of iron that he would never allow to bend. Yet he remembered every moment of his suffering and every occasion of his humiliation, converting each stifled drop to bitterness and bile.

Before being seized by the wasp people Dael had been a mild youth—playful, lighthearted, a joy to his parents, and a happy companion to his twin brother, Zan. He had been known for his smiles. His captors—first the wasp people and afterwards the Noi—changed all that. For the wasp men did not keep him long, but eager for gain, sold him to the Noi, a desert clan.

How had it happened? Dael had quarreled with Zan, and left in anger. After a time, wandering this way and that, he decided to search out the source of Nobla, the river that flowed and bubbled past their home. He and Zan frequently had contemplated this search as a joint project, but now he would go exploring without his stingy brother. All alone, Dael followed Nobla for an afternoon before, as night was falling, he was taken by the marauding wasp men. Disabled by a weapon tipped with a strange venom, the pain of it was so great that he was incapable of resistance—not that it would have done any good. Eventually the poison wore off, but there could be no escaping. He was at their mercy.

For the first time in his life, Dael experienced unkindness. He did not understand the language of the wasp men, and could not even reply to their insults and abuse. There was something about his helplessness that inflamed men who otherwise were not entirely lacking in virtues. Even in his misery Dael could see that his captors lived well, but differently from his own cave-dwelling tribe. They modeled themselves after hornets, carrying stinging spears and building their hollow nests in the trees. They were as comfortable treading on a high limb as walking on the earth below. Looking downward on an enemy, they could swing or climb like apes to attack or defend.

The wasps were a strong, agile, and vigorous people, wise in many arts. And never had Dael seen such a prosperous country. Their weakness was that they were aggressive and quarrelsome, dissipating their strengths and nobler projects through constant disunity. But they were united in their dislike of the "barbarian boy," and had it not been for the sympathy of the women, would have made short work of their prisoner. Dael was tied to a tree while the men argued about what they should do with him. At length they decided to trade him to the Noi for a batch of eagle feathers. Then Dael's troubles began in earnest.

The wasp men had not kept him long, but the Noi did. The trek across desert sands nearly killed Dael, and as soon as the healing women had restored him (that was the first time he saw Lissa-Na), the Noi warriors undertook to break him once again. It became a game among them to see in which creative ways they could abase and humble their captive. Dael bore it all with a silent endurance that thwarted any pleasure and limited their cruel satisfaction. He simply would not show grief.

▼ ▼ ▼

Safely at home during this terrible time, Zan achieved honor by killing a lioness that endangered the clans. He was given a name of honor, Zan-Gah—meaning Zan of the Rock—because he had shown himself so stalwart and brave. But Zan-Gah was tormented by the loss of his twin, and went to look for him. That was a dangerous quest, and Zan nearly died searching the hostile land. Meanwhile, Dael suffered whole years of imprisonment and savage abuse before his twin brother could discover where he was.

If Lissa-Na had not come to love the imprisoned boy, he would have died in his cage; but she helped him survive, and it was she who would secretly release him. However, before the brothers could get away together, Dael slaughtered one of his Noi enemies, crushing his skull with a single blow. *Kind-hearted Dael a killer?* It was over before Zan could do anything to stop the horrific act. Lissa-Na, who had let Dael go, would certainly be held responsible for the killing. So she had to leave too.

The escape of Zan, Dael, and Lissa, rendered more urgent by the gruesome dead body at their feet, proved possible only because of Noi superstition. The Noi were terrified of twins. Swift warriors pursued Lissa and the brothers, but when they saw a "double man" they retreated as from double devils. They had not known that their prisoner was one of an identical pair.

In the progress of their flight, the three were soon taken captive again, not by the Noi, but by their old foes—the wasp people. They were put in seclusion, and would have been hurled headlong to their deaths in a deep abyss but for a nighttime rescue by the gigantic Chul. The uncle of Zan and Dael, Chul once again proved himself faithful and strong—and wise when wisdom was required. He easily snapped the bars of their pen, and off they sped! Still, only with much difficulty did the fugitives return to their home. Only by facing much danger did Zan and his clansmen repel the wasp men's subsequent invasion of their lands. When the fight finally was over,

Zan-Gah was a hero; and Dael, it was plain to see, was much changed from his former self.

▼ ▼ ▼

A year or two of peace and convalescence followed. Dael and Lissa-Na married, and soon Lissa was with child. What happiness! The moon itself never looked on water as Dael's eyes lingered on his pregnant wife. With eager anticipation he watched Lissa grow and her time approach. All of Dael's sorrows were converted to joys, his deep psychic wounds gradually healing.

Lissa-Na appeared to Dael's people (the Ba-Coro) to have come from a different world—but they liked her. Her intelligence was remarkable, so that she easily untangled what could seem the most knotty problem, making the old men wonder. Her startling beauty rendered her unpopular with some of the women at first, but she was eventually recognized for the healer she was. Her very name meant Healer, and her skill was impressive.

Then in childbirth, Lissa-Na died, and Dael's heart died with her. Lissa's sprightly distractions had kept Dael from his memories, enticing him from all the horrors of his past. How gently and with what exquisite tenderness she had coaxed him from his sorrows! She had fed him when he was hungry, nursed him when he was sick, and relieved him when he was oppressed. She had visited him in his agonized moments, and loved him when he could not love himself. And suddenly she was gone.

Her death was horrible. Childbirth screams echoed from the damp cave sanctuary—forbidden to men—

where women bore their young. Lissa's baby finally came out like a fish, took one look at the world, and died. The mother followed an hour after. News was brought to Dael by a woman whose face was ever after painful for him to see. Lissa-Na never once had seen Dael cry, but now his eyes were wet and his face was swollen with grief, like a bawling child. His loss crushed his manhood more than all of his former miseries. After a while he was quieted, until soft and tender memories, rushing upon him, caused him to mourn his loss anew with heartfelt tears.

Lissa's red hair was still flaming when they laid her in a shallow grave. It had been her glory, and now, framing her ashen face and spreading down her neck and shoulders, it made a cushion for her dead baby. A neat layer of flat stones was placed on the grave to prevent hungry animals from digging up the corpses. Dael would have built a mountain of stone in her remembrance, but that sort of honor was reserved for men. It was not customary for a woman's grave. A barrow would keep her spirit alive instead of allowing her to return to the earth of which she was a part.

▼ ▼ ▼

Afterwards, Zan-Gah saw the change—saw the dark nimbus descending over his brother. Dael ceased speaking. He gazed into empty space for long, unexplained periods, or at the fire, as if he were seriously contemplating throwing himself into it. He would not eat, and devoted himself entirely to brooding ruminations occasionally punctuated by facial twitches and wrathful expressions that came and went like glimmers of lightning in a storm-blackened sky.

The climax came suddenly. Well past the middle of the night, Zan felt a shaking of his shoulder as he slept, and then an impatient foot kicking at him. Instinctively grabbing for his spear, he looked up and saw the orange glow of a torch, and as his eyes adjusted to the invading light he recognized his brother's ghastly face. Zan understood at once what was happening. Dael's dangerous brow was furrowed, and the vein of his forehead bulged under the old scar. Zan had not seen that expression for some time. His twin's teeth were clenched, and his eyes darted nervously back and forth. His every motion expressed a profound agitation, and Zan knew that what he had been dreading had come.

"It is time, Zan. Let us go!"

"Where? It's dark!"

"I want to find where the river comes from." In the orange light Dael looked like a priest or a magician who mumbles his incantations to invisible spirits. He was scary.

Thoroughly alarmed, Zan leapt to his feet. He knew what it meant. It meant that Dael could not endure his own thoughts and needed to escape—anywhere! It meant that he could not bear to be stationary. Even now Dael was pacing up and down like a madman.

"I'm sleeping, Dael," Zan said. "I'm not going anywhere, and neither should you." He started to lie down. Dael kicked at him again.

"Then I must go alone?" Dael's face was frightful with emotion. He turned to leave.

"No, wait," Zan said. "I'll go. But call Rydl too. And wait a little for the sun. We can't go in the dark!" Zan was stalling.

"What good is Rydl in manly matters?"

"Still, I want him to come. What about Chul?"

"No."

Fortunately, dawn would soon arrive. Even in the dark of night Zan was unable to restrain Dael's urgent impulsion. Rydl approached, and at a glance comprehended the situation. That was why Zan wanted him around. Rydl was quick to grasp things. And he was a great friend; Zan never had a better. Rydl did not want to go who-knew-where in the middle of the night, but in a whisper Zan begged him to assist in controlling his brother. In his present state Dael was apt to walk off a cliff—or jump off.

A new idea lit—or rather darkened—Dael's face. "The wasp people have been quiet. They are planning something. We cannot live with this danger." Even in his better days, those who knew Dael avoided mentioning either the wasp people or the Noi in his presence.

"Which is it to be, Dael, the river or the wasp people?"

"*Come! Come!*" was all Dael replied.

Zan wished that he could get his brother to lie down and go to sleep. Bed would be balm to him, but never had

Dael seemed so disinclined to rest. Zan tried to reason with him: "What do you seek, Brother? You don't even know where you are going."

"They are like serpents waiting to strike. They must be destroyed before they have done their mischief," Dael responded abstractedly, seemingly unaware of his brother's question.

"Let me get some things," Zan said quietly. From his appearance, Dael might actually have undertaken, all alone, the destruction of the wasp people. "Do you have everything ready for a journey?" Zan asked. Zan knew he didn't.

Suddenly, Dael was rushing about, gathering supplies as if it had only just occurred to him that one could not travel without supplies. He seemed more interested in weapons than water or food.

By now, Pax was awake. "Where are you going, Husband?" she asked. Zan nodded toward Dael's hyperactivity, and she too immediately understood. She tried to say something calming to Dael, but it was as if he did not even see her.

The sun was coming up when Dael, Zan, and Rydl departed—and Pax went with them.

2 PAX

When Zan's wife came along on the strange and vague quest that Dael had begun, she came spear in hand. That was most unusual for a people whose women never carried weapons. In the Ba-Coro clan, as in most tribal societies, the roles of men and women were clearly defined and strongly separated. Only the men carried spears. Men fought the battles and hunted the game; the women did not. But Pax *did* hunt, to the consternation of the males, and she was very good at it, as her grandfather Aniah had been.

Many people loved that aged, sinewy leader, but none more than this grandchild. When Pax was nine, she began secretly following him as he hunted (at that time Aniah always went out alone), doing what he did, stepping as he stepped, and shadowing him like a ghost. She was eleven before Aniah discovered that, as he was stalking the deer, he himself was being stalked. If he had not suddenly fallen—a rare event for the still-agile man—Aniah would not have seen her. When Pax impulsively rushed forward to aid him, he was amazed at her presence. He demanded to know what the child was doing there, and in her soft-spoken explanation it gradually came out that she had been tracing his steps for two years.

Now Aniah was amazed indeed! He, who had no equal in stealth, had been outdone by this little girl! He had gone into the woods a hundred times, and she had always been a few steps away, watching him! Aniah was a thoughtful man. He reflected for a few days on what had happened. When he went out next he invited Pax along—and every time thereafter. He taught her each secret skill that he had—how to use her eyes, nose, and ears, and how to move more quietly than the animal she trailed. In a little while she was able to track even a beetle by the footprints it left in the dust.

Pax brought down her first deer unaided, and dragged it forth with difficulty as it panted its last. For Aniah there was a certain sorrow in it, not only because it seemed so unfit for a young girl, but because she was so like the doe she had speared. Pax was slender-boned, graceful, and delicate, with large, dark eyes that sparkled with moisture and betrayed a trace of timidity. She whispered something in the dying animal's ear, and so did Aniah. They carried it home together.

None of this was received well by the men of the clan (although many of the women secretly rejoiced). At first they even refused to eat the flesh of an animal attained so much in violation of their established ways. But in time Pax's activity was better accepted and she was granted a degree of latitude, mainly because of the great respect her grandfather commanded; but also, as it turned out, because she was exceedingly good at hunting. Aniah, called the greatest hunter who ever lived, was very old, and becoming more and more rheumatic. He had to reduce his exertions. Zan, whose name meant Hunter, was not especially skilled, although he was as adept as the other men of the clan. Who now became the greatest hunter of the Ba-Coro? No one would admit it, yet everyone knew: it was Pax, a girl.

▼ ▼ ▼

Pax was twelve years old when she was given in marriage to Zan-Gah. She was not consulted in the decision. Pax knew her duty and made no objection. She was not really unhappy about it, only a little scared. Zan-Gah was several years older than she, and was already considered a great man of the clan. Everybody seemed to admire him, and some loved him too. She trusted her parents' judgment, and was inclined to like the young hero who was to be her mate. She recalled that when the elders had met in council, Zan had insisted on the inclusion of women—something that never had happened before.

It was marriage itself that Pax objected to, not the man her family had chosen. It appeared a form of slavery to her; and a look at the women of her tribe laboring away at their chores did not dispel that impression. Despite her inherent outward grace, Pax was not inwardly peaceful. The fire of rebellion burnt in her—against her subjugation, her sex, and all its restrictions. She was being handed over to Zan like a haunch of venison or an object of purchase. Would he consider that she was his property? She could not accept that!

It was well after the ceremony that she discovered Zan had no intention of ruling over her; and from that time on Pax blossomed. Far from objecting to her masculine hunting activities, Zan encouraged them, obviously full of admiration for her skill. To Zan, light-stepping Pax was an artist or an elf. She was pretty too, although she seemed not to know it. Gradually Pax realized that Zan-Gah, respected by all, respected her as no less than his equal. He was the one male who ever had done so. Only with this realization did something special grow between them. Only then did Pax surprise her husband with strange and unexpected love-behaviors. Only then could they truly become friends.

▼ ▼ ▼

Among those whom Pax admired, Lissa-Na stood high. In addition to her exotic beauty, Lissa possessed many skills. She could make rope, unknown to the Ba-Coro before her coming, by twisting fibers. She made food taste better by adding unusual herbs; and she was wise in the knowledge of medicines. Her nature, like Pax's, was gentle and restrained, her voice low and beguiling as music. Nor was Pax the only one who looked up to her. One admirer even tried to dye her hair with berry juice to match Lissa-Na's—with unfortunate results.

Although older than Pax, Lissa-Na was disposed to receive her friendship, especially because Lissa was married to Zan's brother, Dael. They immediately took to each other, and were soon trading confidences as good friends will. But Pax's sharp eyes discovered something one day that ended the attachment. It was an odious secret that set her whole body trembling. *Her husband loved Lissa-Na!* Zan could not conceal it, however much he tried. Pax saw how his eyes followed Lissa's movements and remained on her longer than they should. She knew that Zan and Lissa had formerly spent time and faced dangers together, and her jealousy was roused. She began to watch them when they were in each other's presence, and the suspicion was confirmed: Zan loved Lissa more than her. It was their embarrassment in each other's presence that betrayed them, rather than overt attentions.

Friendship turned to frost, and Lissa, who was very perceptive, easily guessed the reason. Now Pax hated her rival, and she tried to hate Zan too; but her hatred did not last long. Suddenly something unexpected and deeply shocking occurred. Even at the height of Pax's anger, as she was wondering whether she should confront Zan with the thing that so much troubled her, Lissa-Na died. Lissa had seemed so triumphantly beautiful and invulnerable. Now Pax's friend, her enemy, the baby, Zan's secret—all disappeared in spasms of agony. Pax could not help being glad—and she detested herself for it.

She felt far more justified in her dislike of Dael. Unlike his twin, Dael did not treat her as his equal, and in fact rarely lost an opportunity to remind her that, in his view, she was not his equal or that of any man. With the iron rigidity that was his character, Dael, more than most, clung to the firm codes of separation that so much galled Zan's wife. He frequently would throw jibes at "women who thought themselves men" or "spear-bearing females," and there had quickly grown between the two something approaching hatred. Dael scoffed at her invasion of male occupations, and Pax at what she considered Dael's dull-minded rigidity. She tried to keep the peace, but it was not only the usual criticism, which many of their tribesmen shared; it was the continual goading, born of an irrational hostility, that would never allow the issue to die.

Nevertheless, when, in the middle of the night, Pax saw the wild agitation of Dael's eyes and the restless instability of his bearing, she felt that it was her duty to calm him if she could. His animosity made her success unlikely. Should she join the group that was so suddenly leaving when her involvement might trouble Dael even more? Pax's conflict lay in the fact that she loved Zan and wanted to help him, while at the same time she was deeply at odds with his twin brother. It was a difficult position, but she went along. Dael, utterly obsessed with his own objectives, seemed completely unaware of her presence.

3 THE BRIDGE

In their childhood, before Zan and Dael had hair on their chins or enemy blood on their hands, in those boyish days when everything seemed new, they had promised themselves a trip up the river Nobla to find out where it came from. It had been mere curiosity then; now it was a fevered obsession in Dael's mind, and Zan was dragged along because he cared about his brother and feared for him.

Nobla's path led them to the Hru camp, where the brothers Oin and Orah lived. Dael had long since made their acquaintance, and dominated the relationship. There was something in Dael's magnetic personality that evoked both fear and favor; and when he called, the two put down their joints of meat, rose, and followed him without question, snatching up their weapons. A third youth arose unbidden and followed Zan.

Zan distrusted Oin and his younger brother Orah. They had attacked him with rocks once and Zan had run them off; but Zan bore no grudge for that encounter. Oin and Orah did! Zan could guess as much by the stony faces they wore in his presence. Moreover, they had always resented

Zan's charity: for when the Hru were starving, Zan had sustained them with a rabbit he had killed with his sling. The small gift had saved the tribe when its men had been too weak with hunger to hunt for their own food—when their faces were gaunt with starvation and their ribs stood out on their wasted bodies. But proud people often resent a helping hand. Oin and Orah, especially the elder, felt a secret shame that they had been so helpless and so much in Zan's debt. Some would have gratefully befriended Zan for his kindness, but humiliated people are rarely thankful. Zan could sense their unspoken hostility. They would be Dael's men, not his.

Having called up the two Hru brothers, Dael turned abruptly westward, leaving the river behind as if it had never existed nor occupied a fixed place in his imagination. Another obsessive urge took ascendancy in his mind: He would find, would *destroy*, the wasp men. All of his furious energies were now focused on that single thought. Forgetting Nobla entirely, he marched to the west with an animal's loping stride, on each side a Hru brother struggling to keep up.

Since they had decisively defeated the wasp men in battle almost three years earlier, the Ba-Coro had not heard from them, and knew nothing of their disasters. Dael, charged with an irrational passion, longed for revenge and the flow of enemy blood. Zan also wanted to pay the wasp people a visit, but with very different aims. First he wanted to do what he could to restrain his brother and to keep him from being killed or killing himself—a fear that had fretted him for some time.

But the question was well raised: What *had* become of the wasp warriors and all their aggressive ways? It was not in their warlike nature to quietly swallow defeat without reprisal. Perhaps they were planning an invasion at the very time that relative ease and a foolish security opened the Ba-Coro to a surprise attack. Nor was the sling weapon Zan had invented, which had played a large part in their great victory, difficult to imitate. Maybe the wasps had figured out how it was made and how it worked, so that they would be as strongly armed as Zan's people. It would not hurt to reconnoiter, if only it could be done quietly—and *sanely*.

There was something else. The wasp people dwelled in the most delightful and fruitful region Zan had ever seen. He called it the Beautiful Country. It was a paradise—or would have been had not those wasp-devils occupied it! Game and fish were abundant to the point of superfluity. Fruit fell from the trees. A long, slender, and graceful cascade supplied fresh water, and there was no sight fairer than the mirror lake into which it thundered. Zan had been a slave there for a full year, and yet his life in the Beautiful Country had been easy—easier than at home! Zan confessed to himself that he had remained with the wasp people as long as he had because he loved their land. He wanted to see it again, and was not averse to the adventure—if only Dael had been himself! Maybe the morning air would cool the mental fever that was driving him.

Chul, the twins' gigantic uncle, and a good companion for such a dangerous trip, had not been invited. Dael, so fierce and certain in his likes and dislikes, did not take to this ungainly man and did not want him along. Chul had not been asleep, and had heard his name mentioned, followed by Dael's decisive "No." Perhaps his feelings were hurt, so he turned over again and tried to go back to sleep. But after a time he got up, reached for his weapons, and followed the group from a distance, carefully keeping his great bulk hidden from their view, and stepping as lightly as Aniah ever had when on the trail of a grunting boar.

▼ ▼ ▼

The road is always easier when you know where you are going. Dael had his destination fixedly in mind, but he depended on Zan to find the way. Thus he was under Zan's galling control to some extent, and Zan was able to restrain his brother's manic energies. Dael's slumbers were agitated. He tossed and groaned and wept in his sleep. But always he was up with the sun, restless and impatient to advance. He did not care if he had eaten or drunk. Oin and Orah followed him like servants, and indeed they provided Dael with the nourishment he needed; else he could have gone hungry.

On the fifth day Dael awoke in a calmer temper, like a raging river that has gone down in the night. (Zan was to learn in time how radically his brother's moods could change.) The wildness left Dael's eyes, and he even began to converse like a rational man. But when Zan questioned him about the trip, it was clear that he would not change his destination or his ferocious objective. He was more capable of making plans, however. Zan watched Dael carefully, determined to respond as the need arose to his turbulent and unpredictable impulses. All he could do was wait and watch and be there for his brother. He could not dissuade him.

The grasslands were full of rabbits. Pax managed to sneak up on one and seize it in her bare hands (such was her skill), bringing it to the men and dropping it at Dael's feet. Had no one but she hunted game, the small band would have had an ample supply of fresh meat. Dael grunted, ate of the roasted animal greedily, and gave Pax no thanks. Zan, however, found a moment to whisper close in her ear how fortunate he considered himself "to have a hunter in the family." He murmured something else besides that made Pax blush with pleasure. Dael, noticing her change, nearly spat in disgust. Dael did not talk to women except to give orders, and, somehow, did not recall ever having whispered to a woman in his life. "What was there to whisper?" he thought.

▼ ▼ ▼

The bridge the wasp men had built over the chasm was still in place, which surprised Zan. In their final retreat, the wasp warriors had been too dazed by defeat and too hard pressed to think about dismantling this single passage connecting the two warring countries. In the many intervening months they had ample opportunity to cut themselves off from their victorious enemies. Why had they not?

"You see! They plan an attack! That is why they kept the bridge," Dael roared. "But we will be the attackers and drink their blood, not they ours!" And his eyes lit up with their latent fire. Zan looked at him uneasily. For all his desire to see the Beautiful Country, Zan had been hoping that there would be no crossing. Then they all could have gone home again. But there it was—a well-made span, consisting of a straight timber and two rails—opening the way like an invitation to any who dared to ignore the stupefying plunge beneath.

Dael and his Hru friends made their way across the bridge with more caution than bravado. Rydl, who was comfortable with heights, hopped across on one foot, making a mocking display of his acrobatic skill. The bridge shook, scaring everybody, especially Oin and Orah, who began to whimper aloud. Rydl could have crossed this bridge with his eyes closed. His people, the wasps, lived in trees, and it was high above the earth that he had first learned to walk, harnessed in his infancy for safety.

Zan and Pax went next. Pax was afraid of high places, and she clung to Zan's hand while Dael and his companions snickered at her weakness. Catching a word or two of their scorn, Pax bore up, and even paused to peer into the vertiginous depths. White birds were screaming around their nests, feeding their young, which cheered her a little when she got used to the height. She paused to pick up a fallen feather and tucked it in her buckskin garment close to her bosom. "Do you like it, Zan?" Yes, he did. A few more steps and they were on the other side.

▾ ▾ ▾

Days were passing. The earth beneath their feet grew gradually redder and rockier as the group approached the land of red rocks. Zan and Rydl remembered the place well, but no amount of familiarity could diminish the wonder of it, or the actual experience of the looming and fantastic towers of stone. Amazing palisades topped sheer red cliffs that flanked the broad passage of the valley; and a crimson brook, the only source of life in the parched red region, wandered through a maze of scattered boulders.

Rydl was the first to recognize the cave dugout—only one of many—where he and Zan had formerly taken shelter. When he pointed it out, Dael immediately saw the skull configuration, as if he had been looking for it, and called it to the attention of his two Hru friends. The cluster of rocks and pockets looked like a skull! Three pits made hollow eyes and nose, and an irregular ridge of stones just beneath formed a ghastly smile. Oin and Orah shuddered, and Pax was not gladdened when she identified a second skull formation in the irregularities of the cliff on the other side.

Zan had no fear of these constructions of the imagination, but he worried about the effect they might have on his companions, who were already exchanging apprehensive words. But Dael, exultant, was almost trembling with joy. "Yes," he cried, "these walls of rock speak the truth! Death is here and death is there. The very stones proclaim it! The valley will run red with blood like this unnatural river. Let us drink from it now in anticipation of our triumph and their destruction." Oin and Orah forced themselves to smile. Pax looked at Zan, and Zan looked with fear, not at the skulls, but at his brother.

4 THE HIVE

After a night's rest in the cave-like hollow, which was the mouth of the "skull," they were on their way. The great distances gradually were left behind. It proved easier, safer, and even faster to travel in a group. Zan knew exactly where to go as they approached the mountainous region that was the wasp people's abode. A pair of foothills somewhat separated from the others told him the path.

Rydl was both desirous and reluctant to return to his home. He had been away for several years, and longed to see his father and visit his mother's grave (although he never knew her alive). His departure from home had been sudden. An atmosphere of suspicion made it dangerous for him to stay, for he had once helped Zan-Gah, an enemy, and his father had guessed as much. If he now returned with Zan and other strangers, the suspicion would be confirmed and his life would be in danger. Rydl decided to stay back a little distance for a while.

"Why don't you keep company with the great booby who has been dogging our steps all this time?" Dael suggested, casting a thumb over his shoulder. Dael alone had noticed that Chul was following them, and now brought the fact to the attention of the group. Finally seeing Chul, who perceived that he had been spotted, Rydl decided to act on Dael's advice and ran to join the blushing giant. Chul and Rydl camped separately and built a fire while the others went forward toward the bluish hills.

Arriving at a clear space, Zan suddenly recognized the red tower of stone that looked so curiously like his brother that, at a distance, he had once called out to it. The sculptured rock was like the skulls of the red cliffs: one saw something that was not there. Yet, how much Dael resembled (not only physically!) that unfeeling column—rigid and unyielding, hard—and how different it was from what Dael formerly had been!

It was just at that moment, as Zan was ruefully recalling how he once had mistaken the stone pile for his missing brother, that he smelled a faint odor, which would become more prominent as the group advanced. Wafted by the wind was the sickening smell of a dead animal, and before long it was as if the whole region were infected. A shift of the breeze took the odor away again, only to bring it back a while later with increased strength and foulness. Chul and Rydl, who had changed their minds after eating and decided to catch up with the others, noticed it too. Chul possessed a keen nose, and had detected the smell even the night before.

They came together as they reached a point above the dwellings of the wasp people. Silently and with great caution, the band climbed the ridge overlooking that glorious region which Zan called the Beautiful Country.

Zan, Pax, and Rydl, the only ones among them who had any sense of beauty, drank in the loveliness of the land. Beyond the neatly arranged huts the trees were already in bloom, reflected in the mirror surface of the pure and ever-freshening lake; while in the distance a stream fell from a great height to replenish it. Then, even as they gazed in wonder at the gratifying sight, the wind shifted, and the smell was there again, fouling for one sense what was fair to another—a putrid odor, fetid and unwholesome. Chul snorted like a bull. Dael knew the smell (although he would not say whence his knowledge came), and seemed even to welcome the stench of death—for death it had to be. Somewhere nearby there were rotting corpses—but whose?

The wasp people, Zan recalled (for he had been their captive many months), had no feeling for the beauty of their land—only for its richness and ease of gathering. He knew, however, that they abhorred rotten meat, and would not tolerate its presence. *But where were they?* Their huts were intact on the ground, and their hive-like nests hung undisturbed from the lofty branches above. Rydl said that something was wrong, and Zan feared a trap. Perhaps their sentinels had spotted the band and were lying in wait until the invaders approached too near for escape. Then they would swarm out of their nests and it would all be over.

Dael was readying his spear with its blade of flint. Zan could see that it would be difficult to hold him back for very long, and wished he could tie him to a tree for his own safety.

Something had to be done to resolve them of the situation, so Zan threw a stone, which made a rattling noise.

There was no response.

Creeping closer, with his friends directly behind, he threw a larger one at the closest of the huts. These were bulbous, hive-like structures built of branches sealed with tar, and covered with bark and leaves. Standing up, Zan flung a rock with his powerful sling directly into the round door of the hollow hive.

Nothing.

There were no fires or any sign of life at all. And still the fetid, loathsome odor assailed their nostrils.

Zan urged his companions to watch and wait. Best to be cautious. But after a long hour spent observing the lifeless scene—a period of complete silence—Dael could be restrained no longer. Ignoring the others and his own safety, he rushed forward with a wild yell and plunged his spear into the wasp-hut as though it were a living creature.

The rest of the group had no choice but to charge on the run to second Dael's attack. There could be no hiding any more; it was fight or flee. Chul, in the forefront, brandished his spear and roared like a wild animal. But the wasp warriors made no answer. The continuing silence made it plain at last that, wherever the wasp people were, they were not there. Men, women, and children—all were gone. No movement whatever disturbed the quietude, except for a dusty wind brushing against the rough, dry walls of the forsaken village.

The largest of the huts was the regal seat of their mightiest elder. Jaga was his name. Zan remembered him well—intelligent, quick, and savage as any wild man. Once, during the period of Zan's internment there, Jaga had detected a note of rebellion in his younger brother's voice. Quick as lightning, he had struck the youth with his club. He then flung the body into a fire to roast as a charred example to any who might attempt to defy him. That was the sort of man he was. Many hated him; all feared him—and obeyed without question. Not one dared to utter a word of protest against the barbaric murder.

How often Zan had done Jaga and his large family a slave's service when he had been their captive! Where were they now? Zan resolved to enter the soundless hut, slowly, cautiously. Little was visible within until Zan's eyes adjusted to the semidarkness, but the overpowering odor nearly felled him. Holding his nose, he gradually made something out by the sparks of bright light penetrating a few cracks in the nest's structure.

It was the most ghastly sight he ever had seen. The earthen floor was strewn with decaying corpses. Rotting and shriveled bodies were everywhere, swarming with flies. And seated on his throne of power was the corpse of Jaga, still erect in the place of honor reserved for a chief. His once imperial face and vigorous body were now horribly desiccated, his skull eyeless, and his mouth wide open to reveal ivory teeth ringing the dark putrescence. He still wore his beautiful fur pelt, and held in his skeleton grip the scepter spear that marked him for command. Even in death, Zan thought, Jaga would not relinquish his authority. Despite the horrible change that death had made, Zan could still recognize his kingly features, and even whispered his name: "Jaga?" In answer, a swarm of wasps issued from Jaga's throat and hovered around what once had been his not unhandsome face.

Zan turned to flee, and received another shock. Silhouetted against the light of the oval opening and barring his exit was the startling apparition of an old woman. So haggard, grotesque, and emaciated she was, and so sudden was her appearance, that Zan jumped when she spoke and, for a moment, the hairs stood up on his head.

"Who are you, and how do you dare to disturb this place of death?" she demanded. She looked as if she herself might have risen from the number of decaying corpses, coming back to life to confront the young intruder. Her hoarse words, which seemed fashioned from a gust of wind, were in the wasp men's language, which Zan had learned during his captivity there.

"I am Zan-Gah. I have returned to visit this country and..."

"Oh ho, the dumb boy speaks!" The woman recognized Zan as their "idiot" slave of former days. Zan had played that part well when his survival made it necessary. The hag disgorged a dry, cackling laugh. Zan knew her. It was Hurnoa, a once prominent woman of the tribe, who had defended him from Naz, his sadistic guard. Although Zan had been compelled to serve her, he remembered Hurnoa as a just and even kind supervisor. How horribly was she changed! Where once she had been plump and prosperous, she was now stooped and gaunt, her skeleton more prominent than the dried flesh affixed to it. Her once strong and capable hands resembled the roots of unearthed trees, and her former ringing and authoritative voice was as shriveled as her visage. The thick ebony hair had become as white as ashes and so thin that it scarcely covered her scalp. No trace of her former dignity remained. Zan gazed at her almost in horror.

"What...has...happened here?" Zan demanded at last, ushering the old woman into the bright open light. Zan's band, surprised that anyone was there at all, gaped at her as though she were a freak of nature. Chul averted his nose, and Dael marked her with cruel eyes, readying his spear. Pax and Rydl moved closer to Zan, while Oin and Orah huddled behind Dael for protection.

But Hurnoa would present no threat. Weakened by sickness, starvation, and an evident weariness of life, she sat down on the dusty ground. A bonfire once had burned in the very spot she chose, and scattered relics of the long-extinct blaze remained. Hurnoa sat among the ashes. The others sat too, forming a ring around her.

5 "WHAT HAPPENED?"

"Yes, young man, I remember you well," she continued in her fractured voice. The gleam in her eyes belied her withered face and body. "I knew you were not the dumb ape you pretended to be, but I held my tongue lest you be chopped to pieces. And you did well to hold yours. Your mind seemed as barren as our western desert, and no one among us feared you."

Zan repeated his question: "What happened?"

Hurnoa paused to assemble her thoughts. Zan's simple question was almost more than she could bear. She looked at the ground and seemed to visibly shrink as she meditated her answer. At last, speaking as if to herself while still looking at the earth, she sighed, "I do not know why the gods decided to destroy us. They began by making us furious, then crazy, then sickened and sick to death. Do you see our hives in the trees above? Every one contains dead bodies. No person has survived. Not one—saving myself."

"What, not one?" Rydl exclaimed, and his mouth went dry. He tried to absorb what her words meant. "Not one?

What has done this?" He thought of his father whom he both feared and missed. He would never see him after all, nor make peace with him.

Zan was translating to the group. Dael listened, but was too baffled to speak. Things were not falling out as he had planned!

Hurnoa continued, more conscious of her audience: "The land we inhabit is rich. Look around you! Game, fish, and fruits are everywhere. We had no needs. No people were as prosperous as we, and we were so strong that no one dared to attack us. But men are makers of mischief." Hurnoa's exhausted and haggard look became still wearier, and her face more deeply entrenched as she proceeded, until she looked as if she might wither away entirely. "Our clans despised one another and fought on any pretext, while the women cowered—always fearful of murder or abduction. Our children were not safe either. They might disappear at any time, never to be seen again. And so the sweetness of our land was ever turned sour by its inhabitants.

"Jaga, our chief, had three brothers (tall, handsome men!) whom he sought to make chieftains over the other clans. To this end he was always plotting, and when the youngest declared that he did not wish to rule over unwilling subjects, Jaga struck him dead with his club. No one should dare, he said, to challenge his decisions instead of obeying. I can still see the comely young body roasting on the fire! The day afterwards, Jaga was weeping and roaring over his deed. He had power over all—except himself. And so he wept, but the dead cannot be brought back to life.

"Later, Jaga engendered a plan to unite our clans under his rule by making war elsewhere (it mattered not where) with himself as leader. The idea of battle makes men crazy, and they who were at each other's throats at that very time diverted their thoughts to a great invasion. Almost at once the warriors were beating their shields with their spears and shouting the name of Jaga! Jaga! as if he were their greatest friend—he who never felt a moment's sympathy for them. Did they think, once victorious in war, that Jaga would prove a kind ruler—the monster who had murdered his own brother?" Hurnoa, sickly and weak, paused to catch her breath. Zan was translating her words as well as he could.

"Jaga's target was the people of the east, beyond the great cleft in the earth—your people. We told ourselves that you were inferior and only fit to be slaves, and that victory with our poisoned weapons was a certainty. How eagerly the men readied themselves for battle!" Hurnoa closed her eyes for a moment, too pained to continue, and slowly shook her head. "What devil is it that makes men prefer war to peace?" she inquired, more of herself than her audience. "Maybe life was too easy! Men who do not have to struggle in order to eat, men with idle time and over-abundant energy, turn their minds to war and conquest. I don't know why. And yet we, the attackers, needed nothing that your people had. And you were far away! Why should we seek you? Our minds were sick before our bodies were."

Zan urged the old woman to eat something from his supplies and resume her tale after she felt stronger.

But she could hardly chew the coarse food Zan gave her, and soon put it aside. After a while she continued unbidden: "Jaga led an army of our warriors, eager for battle and thinking themselves invulnerable; and a single man overthrew the entire attack! We were told he was a giant. Perhaps it was that huge fellow you have with you." She pointed a bony finger at Chul. "He hurled down the bridge spanning the abyss, cutting off our forces and sending them home unsatisfied."

"Yes," Chul responded, wiping his nose with his hairy fist. "I sent them home, and I wish they had stayed there. I have other things to do besides fighting and killing wild men." Hurnoa did not understand his words, only the gruffness of his tone.

"What vexation and rage they brought back with them! Eager for war, they could only war on each other. The alliance fell apart more quickly than it was formed, and Jaga, who was blamed for everything, had to surround himself with armed guards to prevent his assassination.

"Jaga was beaten for a time, but Crawf, the oldest of his brothers, began to buzz about. His plan was to bring the warriors together under his leadership by promising a new, successful campaign. Jaga was not happy with his brother's ambition, but decided to allow him to build the alliance with the intention (I am sure) of getting rid of him after he had done the work of war. But the gods had other plans.

"You know yourself, young man, that at the time you served us we encountered a new, invisible enemy—an evil spirit against whom we were helpless. We sent you away because it was thought that you were the demon, but we discovered otherwise. This spirit rode on every breeze, and if it touched you in the morning, you would be dead by the next evening! Your face, arms, and legs felt as if they were on fire, and before long blood issued from your nose and eyes, and every part of your body. With convulsions and hoarse cries, each victim would grapple with the demon. The swelling was terribly painful, and so disfiguring that members of your own family could hardly recognize you. But before long your agonies would be over, and your family's too! We soon learned—although not soon enough—that the spirit visited anyone who touched the dying. We could hardly dispose of the corpses, and this dreadful smell came to keep the injurious spirit company.

"One of the elders said that the evil came upon us because we were cowards, slow to resume the battle; and the men, both frightened and furious, and anxious to get away from the curse, were more eager to fight than ever. Not many returned, and those who did found death in every hive. But even so desolated, there were those who wanted to seize power from Jaga—who himself was powerless to overcome what had befallen us.

"The bad spirit went away for a time, and the warriors broke into a number of shifting friendships and plotting alliances. The war had not done enough damage! The plague had not left enough stinking bodies! They decided to make more! Elders were killed in their beds and families fought against their own clans, so that corpses were everywhere. The young men were emboldened, and held secret councils. Jaga's enemies could not get at him because he was guarded night and day; so they killed his brothers. Madness! Jaga never hungered for revenge nor plotted its fulfillment with such driving energy! But it came to nothing. Within three days of his brothers' murders the death-tokens appeared, and by the time five days had passed, Jaga and most of his guard were breathed down by the spirit. You saw their corpses just now.

"The ill spirit has finished its work. I do not know why it left me alive to look on nothing but the dead. My family and my people all have perished. I wish I could die too." Tears were making their way down Hurnoa's shrunken cheeks.

"Filthy hag, you will get your wish!" Dael exclaimed, and he might have killed her with his spear if Zan had not intervened.

"Dael! No! This unlucky woman was once kind to me, and may have saved my life."

"She is a wasp and she dies! Terrible old woman! Why should we keep her alive?"

Zan could see that it was useless to reason with his brother. Rydl came to Zan's side to second him, and Chul interposed his bulk. It was the first of many coming confrontations. Meanwhile, the old woman looked directly at Dael and smiled, stretching her palms forward in supplication, as one who welcomes a friend or begs a favor.

Dael, prevented from his purpose, was coldly furious. "I gave you that one"—he pointed at Rydl—"because he is dear to you, although I don't know why." He smiled an ugly, insinuating smile. "But this one is mine."

"What is wrong with you, Dael?" Zan asked. "Do you enjoy killing?" Zan was immediately sorry to have asked that question—because he knew the answer.

Pax, in a tone more gentle than she usually addressed to Dael asked: "Have you lost your mind, Dael?" And she too was sorry to have inquired.

Dael lowered his spear and turned on his heel. "We will see," he muttered, and he walked away.

The confrontation was over. Dael had backed down. Chul, relieved, built a bonfire, and Zan gave some thought to what he wanted to do. He had known many of the dead, and even had pleasant memories of some. Hurnoa and other women had been kind to him, and some few had looked on him with pity as well as mockery when they considered him a speechless fool. Now all were corpses.

Thal, Zan's great father, had taught him to respect the dead. "Their angry spirits will haunt your life and turn it sour, but that is not why you should do them justice. Do it because you would wish it done to you." Justice required that the many bodies should be respectfully disposed of.

Zan had an idea. What would be reverence for Zan would be annihilation for Dael, he thought. Dael longed to destroy, and this could be an opportunity to satisfy his thirst and finally quiet him down. "Dael," he called.

"Here is our fire. Let us purge the demon and destroy the wasp men's nests."

Dael leapt eagerly to the task, beginning with Jaga's putrid house and the other ground structures. The furious blaze drove them back, and as they watched the conflagration from a safe distance, Dael almost danced with glee. Dael loved fire, and delighted in seeing the wasp dwellings burn. The smell of rottenness was now replaced by the acrid stench of burning corpses as crackling fire and rolling smoke erupted from the dens.

The nests suspended in the trees above presented a problem, being deliberately built to be inaccessible; but Dael was not to be deterred. Placing a burning rod between his teeth, he climbed one of the supporting trees and inched out along a heavy limb. Rydl went up after him, but Rydl, having been born in one of these nests, was as used to climbing and swinging as walking on the ground. While Dael struggled to keep his balance, Rydl made a scoffing show of his skill by hopping back and forth on Dael's limb—forty feet above the ground! Dael lay down, clinging to the branch and fearing any shift of balance. Rydl extended a foot, not a hand, to him.

There was no friendship between them. Dael glowered and rose on his own, at last managing to cast his torch into one of the nests. In his captivity, Zan had learned some of the wasp man's skill in climbing, and together the three set every hive ablaze. Those below watched the spectacle. For Hurnoa it was like the end of all, and she stood transfixed. Her whole world had died and was now disappearing in clouds of black smoke.

There were seven separate camps, and it was a labor to bring fire to them. After the first, they knew to destroy the topmost nests before those below, thus avoiding the rising heat and fumes. The dwellings had been fashioned largely of bark and leaves. Because they had been sealed with tar, they burned and smoked furiously in great, roaring spheres of fire. By the time night fell, the spectacular blaze illuminated the lake and surrounding area with an unnatural glow that tinted every object, even the distant granite cliff and its long-descending waterfall. In time the fires waned, but the trees continued to drop bright showers of sparks for a while. All the travelers were tired, and prepared for a night's rest.

As Dael was about to sleep, Zan approached him. "Do not be angry, Dael. You see that our enemies are ashes, and that there is nothing in this land that is not ours. What a victory this is for us!"

Dael refused to be pacified. "Do not cross me again, Brother," Dael replied, not looking at Zan but at the flickering glow on the distant granite cliff. "And do not suppose that you are as strong as I." That was all he said, and Zan departed to join his wife.

By morning, nothing was left of the wasp dens but gray ashes and a few glowing embers. An early breeze took the last of the fetid odor away, and the land was purged of the evil. Except for the scarred trees, all was beautiful and peaceful, and few signs of the holocaust remained.

Zan made a speech: "Friends and kinsmen, we have come here at great risk, ready for a fight that might well have led to our destruction. But spirits—good or evil—have fought for us and undone our enemies. And not a blow was struck by our arms! The land, the Beautiful Country is purified—and it is empty. It is ours! Dael, what do you think? Can we not....*What happened to Dael?*"

All were present but he. No, Hurnoa had disappeared somewhere too! No one knew where they were, and Zan, with fearful misgivings, instructed his group to seek them out without delay.

It took only a few moments for Zan himself to find Dael behind some bushes, conversing peaceably with Hurnoa. But how could that be when Dael hated the old woman and spoke but little, even to his friends? Zan drew closer. A slight smile on his face, Dael was reclining, leaning comfortably on his elbow, and talking softly to her. Then Zan saw. Dael's hands were covered with blood. And it was the seated corpse of Hurnoa that he was quietly addressing.

6 RYDL

When Rydl climbed to the high treetops to flame the wasp men's nests, he felt no joy, as Dael did. For Dael it was a feast of revenge. To Rydl it was a last act of respect for the people who once had been his own. When he came to the dwelling of his father, he could not bring himself to enter. His father was dead now. All he could do was say a prayer and put the putrid hive to the torch.

Rydl was a runaway, but he had hoped to see his father once again, to mend the old divisions that had put them apart, and make peace with his people. That was the dream he was carrying with him since he had left with Zan and the others. He even allowed himself to imagine the joy of his homecoming.

Yet he had never loved his father, and had rarely felt a moment's comfort in his presence. Styg had been a brute, and Rydl learned to fear him at an early age. His gentle mother (he knew all about her) had died when he was born, and Styg, unable to show his grief and anger, had taken both out on the child. Even as a boy Rydl recognized that he should stay out of the way of his father's sudden, violent outbursts; and bore that watchful look of fear that children have when they know they may be struck or abused without reason at any time. Rydl found that when his father was aloft, he had best be on the ground, and that he would be most comfortable above when his father was below. Styg did not understand how he had driven his son away, and angrily resented his sullen coldness. His feelings for his son—an unpredictable mixture of love, perplexity, and hate—only frightened the boy.

When Rydl was nine years old, Styg's brutalities sent him running. By sheer accident, Zan-Gah in his wanderings became the father and brother Rydl so much needed. Zan had found him under the vines, wretched, terrified, and near starvation, and had taken him into his care. Rydl gratefully followed Zan to the point of being an annoyance—trailing his footsteps, singing, talking to himself, and hopping about. But it was Zan's magnificent virtue that he could understand the needs of a troubled, homeless lad, and tolerate his antics. He did not despise Rydl because he was young and weak and in need. The fact was that he liked the silly kid. In return, Rydl was doggedly faithful to the older boy, and in time became that rare thing, a truly loyal friend.

In spite of the difficulties of his childhood, Rydl was a joyful person. Released from his father's persecutions, his mind became active and his heart glad. His happiness showed itself in an unusual restlessness of spirit. He was continually playing, climbing, jumping from rock to rock, chasing a chipmunk, shouting to hear his echo, or simply babbling to the empty air.

But as he grew older, Rydl developed a different restlessness, more of the mind than the body. Now he would shout to the cliffs to see how long it took for his echo to return; and he would wait silently for a chipmunk to appear in order to study its habits. He watched the behavior of ants by the hour—how they moved in predictable ways, or how the red ants instinctively fought the black ones. "People are like that too," he had commented to Zan, and Zan had thought over and remembered Rydl's words.

By that time, Rydl had grown into a tall, slender youth. His face was pretty, almost the face of a young girl, and he had long, graceful, and feminine curls. No one would have guessed, looking at him, the fierceness of the people he had come from. He was noted for his mildness and a strange dreaminess that was ever interrupted by flashes of thought.

Rydl was not like the other lads, although it would be difficult to say how he differed. Perhaps it was his alien origin. He looked at things—often very small things—more closely than necessity seemed to require, giving rapt attention to objects that others did not care to notice at all. And he was always analyzing and inventing. His mercurial mind occupied an entirely separate realm from that of his fellows.

One time he noticed that some seeds had been spilled and were producing feathery sprouts. Over and over Rydl would look at them. He pulled some up and peered at the roots. He tasted them. Then he seemingly forgot all about them. But several days later, Zan noticed that

Rydl was talking to an oak seedling he had plucked up: "I am sorry, little being, to have ended your short life, but I have need of you." He took the plant to the nearby river to wash the dirt off, afterwards studying it almost reverently as if it held an important secret. He split the acorn and examined the new plant's insides, sprout and root. And then he thought about it—and *thought*! Later that afternoon he was observed examining each grain closely in the light before eating it. Three weeks later he was stooping over a small green patch. It was rice, which he had planted. Then he planted squash seeds and watched the vines grow and spread. No one among the Ba-Coro had ever thought of growing anything.

Rydl's ideas were often the object of mockery. He suggested dipping rocks into the wasp poison, combining the advantages of two separate weapons, poisoned spear and sling. Zan pointed out that a sharp poisoned rock might be hard to carry, and everybody laughed. Still, Rydl was long fascinated with the idea of somehow combining the virtues of the sling with those of the spear.

One spring dawn, Rydl was seen placing a pole in the earth to mark where the sun rose; and each day afterwards he noted that it rose in a slightly different place. He marked its rising every ten days. This was Dael's chance to jeer at what he did not understand. Out of spite he kicked down the posts Rydl had carefully set up, and the experiment ended. Another time Rydl drew a map on the ground with a stick. "How can that lump of earth be a mountain?" Oin had scoffed. "And how can that red coal be our campfire?" echoed Orah. "Or that mark a river?"

Only Zan refrained from laughter. Rydl's inventiveness commanded respect, even when his ideas seemed crazy. Besides, sometimes they made sense.

What Rydl had that his fellows lacked was a creative imagination. He occupied a separate world as lively as theirs was stolid and dull. While others plodded on in the same way their fathers had, Rydl, who no longer had a father, was constantly inventing new solutions—or at least asking new questions. Little escaped his notice and his wonder. He alone asked where tongues of fire came from and where they went. He could look at two handfuls of seeds and tell which would taste better. He could guess which way a boar went when the trail was cold. He learned to erect hunting blinds (even Pax had not thought of that), and to put out squash for bait to bring the animal within striking distance.

All of these curious ways were laughed at, mostly in a friendly way. Chul brayed out his laughter too, but Rydl did not mind. He knew Chul was a man of no imagination and liked him anyway. And Chul liked Rydl—not only because Rydl's ingenuity had once saved his life, but for another more basic reason: dullness admires genius. Both had kind hearts, and between such people there is always friendship.

Rydl could do marvelous things—he quickly had learned to spin rope from Lissa-Na—but for some reason, no one seemed to take him seriously. Chul looked at his works in utter puzzlement. Pax was fascinated by his originality, but she was puzzled too. And Dael openly jeered at him. Dael had kicked down the sun-marking poles, and also trampled the patch of green, daring Rydl to do anything about it.

"Do not be concerned, Little Friend," Chul said. (Chul was in the habit of calling Rydl that.) He laid his great, hairy hand on Rydl's shoulder. "You are clever, and being smart is more important than being strong." Dael happened to overhear Chul's words, and imitating his heavy, gravelly speech repeated them in a mocking tone in Rydl's ear: "Being smart is more *important*...Being smart is more *important*...!" And Oin and Orah joined in until they were all tired of it. Rydl dismissed them for the fools they were and walked away.

About that time Rydl began to develop a snare for animals, using a sweet bait that he thought might attract a possum. Their meat was tender and delicious and well worth catching. But when he actually caught one, Dael took it for himself and was eating its roasted flesh by the time Rydl discovered where it went. Rydl's protest met with violence. Dael easily overcame him and pinned his face to the ground.

"Would you like to taste dirt, worm?" he said, twisting Rydl's arm behind his back. "Rydl, the worm. Rydl, the maggot. Go play in the dirt, worm!" And he let him go so he could continue eating his stolen dinner.

Rydl was no coward, but he had long experience with abusive people and knew better than to respond in kind. Practically from the first moment he met him, Rydl was wary of Zan's twin. There was something explosive within Dael that constantly threatened to erupt. It was wisdom, not cowardice to avoid him. Rydl understood that the savage cruelty that had ended Hurnoa's life was the work of a disturbed mind. If there were to be a fight, one of them would die—probably he himself. Nor could he easily bring himself to fight Zan's brother to the death, unless there were no way out.

Yet Rydl had learned to take care of himself. He knew a dozen ways to trip up his enemies, and could quickly invent still more—like the time he gave poison mushrooms to the great louts who tried to kidnap him and ran away while they were vomiting. He was an adept climber, and could escape Dael's anger like a fugitive squirrel if necessary and laugh at him from above.

Never once had Rydl mistaken one twin for the other. Rydl loved Zan and wished he could like Dael too. The harder Dael was on him, the more Rydl sought Zan's company and protection. When alone together they sometimes spoke in the wasp tongue, a dead language to everyone but them: "I know that he is that way," Zan said in the foreign tongue, "but it is not wholly his fault. If only you knew what he was like before his capture, before his ordeal, you might feel sorry for him. He was milder than you are—kind, generous, and always laughing—an entirely different person! I remember how he avoided fishing because he didn't want to hurt the fish! Do not hate him, Rydl. He has suffered so much...and now Lissa's death...and truly I fear he is not in his right mind."

Rydl was pacified, and he went on experimenting and making his traps and tending some new squashes, until Oin and Orah trampled them down.

7 THE TRAP

The antipathy of Rydl and Dael would prove to be a lengthy story. Later on, after the adventurers had returned to their home with the news of the wasp people's destruction, Rydl would begin another project:

There was a girl, about thirteen years old, who had never learned to speak. No one knew why. She was extremely shy and kept to herself as much as she could, apparently ashamed of her impairment. Rydl made it his business to draw her out, and when he had somewhat overcome her timidity, he sat her on a log, pointed to her, and spoke her name: "Sparrow." Then he pointed to himself and spoke his own. Sparrow knew what was expected of her and ran away, but the next day Rydl tried again, and every day afterwards. Her painful attempts to speak, when he finally could get her to try, were almost comic. She could only sputter. Rydl was not discouraged, but continued his efforts for a few minutes every day.

Rydl himself was not a perfect speaker. Being a foreigner, he spoke with an unusual pronunciation, which had frequently opened him to coarse mockery. Actually, despite this flaw, Rydl had a noble command of language that none of his comrades could approach, and a pleasant tone of voice that appealed to many, especially girls. It was this that had attracted Sparrow.

Rydl discovered that Sparrow could sing a little, even if she could not form words, and he guessed that this might be the key to her improvement. When Dael caught Rydl in his efforts, his sneering smile was mixed with a frown of incomprehension. He dismissed them both with laughter—at her for her wordless song, and at him for his accent. "An idiot teaching an idiot," he muttered within Zan's hearing. Zan remembered his own captivity, when he too had been called "idiot," but he said nothing.

Some of the tribesmen assumed that Rydl was in love, and anyone could see that Sparrow was captivated. No one had ever shown her the least attention, and now Rydl was spending time with her every day, and softly singing to her. Soon Sparrow actually sputtered a word or two, and did a little better as time went on. She tried hard because she was in love with her teacher and wanted to please him. Rydl *was* pleased, but he did not return her blossoming affection.

Although Rydl had a loving heart, he had never been in love with a girl. Possibly it was not part of his makeup. Sometimes Rydl would touch Sparrow's lips and cheeks, but it was part of the lesson to him. Not to her! Dael and his companions were soon making singsong jokes at their expense, and imitating Sparrow's wide-eyed look of affection. Dael and his friends were becoming a problem.

Rydl's whole life had been a struggle to survive, yet this had not the least bit affected the sweetness of his character. He was not inclined to violence, but something had to be done about Dael. Why Dael hated him so much was hard to say. Like all of Dael's obsessions, it was ruthless and unshakable. He regarded Rydl's ways as effeminate, which he detested; and Rydl had been born a wasp, which made him one of the enemy in Dael's secret thoughts. But mostly, he disliked Rydl because he could not begin to understand him, and that made Dael doubt himself.

The clash finally came. There was no avoiding it because Dael desired it—and Rydl was ready. An angry exchange of words and Dael was chasing Rydl with his spear. At the first opportunity, Rydl scrambled up a tree and Dael, who did not see him escape, wondered where he went. He looked all around, checking behind tree trunks and in the brushy areas that were choked with dry leaves. As he searched, Dael spied something he wanted, a brilliant blue feather lying on the ground and gleaming in the sunlight. All the Ba-Coro people prized feathers, and this one was a beauty! As he went to get it he stepped in a hole—and the trap was sprung! Dael suddenly found himself helplessly hanging by one leg from a large but supple tree, which bent but did not break under his weight.

The bright feather had been bait. Rydl's large snare worked exactly as the small one had. He descended from his hiding place with three easy swings of his arms, and picked up the feather, idly examining it while Dael dangled. Then seizing the spear, which was lying on the ground, he pointed it directly at Dael's left eye: "You are stronger than I am, but a bear is smarter than you. I could kill you right now, but why bother? You will soon enough kill yourself." Then he said: "*Being smart is more important than being strong.*" He threw down Dael's spear and left him hanging there until Oin and Orah found him and cut him down.

8 A DECISION

The death of Hurnoa at the hands of a loved brother had deeply troubled Zan, but there was nothing he could do to bring the old woman back. The dead cannot be returned to life again. It was time for the living to go home. Hopefully, travel and conversation would help bring Dael to himself. There was no practical way to punish him, but Zan hoped the killer would repent in time and regain the gentle humanity he had once possessed.

As the travelers progressed to their cavern home, they thought a good deal about Hurnoa, but none spoke of her. Rather, they talked at length about the fate of the wasp men and the mysterious spirit that had destroyed them. Discussion then turned to the wasp men's country, and as they passed from one difficult terrain to another, the rich land they had left behind seemed more and more desirable. The remembrance of the fetid odor of death did not quickly leave their minds; but who could resist the temptation of a place where food was always plentiful and the eye was always delighted? Pax, her white feather still attached to her scanty clothing, sidled close to Zan and said that she hated to leave the Beautiful Country.

Zan had been quiet and thoughtful (he almost always was), but broke his silence when Pax spoke because she had touched on the very thought that was occupying his mind. "Why are some lands so much more pleasant and generous than others?" he mused aloud. "And why do we remain tied to the hostile place we dwell in now? Game is always scarce. Nobla, our river, dries up in the summer, and we are forced to move up and down, always in search of something to eat. We follow the herds, ever just beyond our reach, and almost become a wandering herd ourselves, foraging for food."

For once Dael, who walked a little in front of his brother, was responsive to his thoughts: "We will inherit the wasp men's land. We have but to move there and take it for ourselves! We will eat their game and pick their fruit, and sometimes we will step on their ashes!"

The journey went quickly. Before they reached the deep chasm, everyone in the group was talking eagerly about a move—except for Rydl. That fair country had once been his home, and his mind churned at the thought of a permanent return to the place where all whom he had known were gone. For Rydl it was a land of ghostly memories, and he was glad to be leaving it. How could he ever forget the smell of his father's corpse, or live untroubled in the place where so many kinsmen had perished? But the idea of moving was so much taking hold that Zan began planning what he would say to the elders of the Ba-Coro.

One of these elders was Chul. (Chul was not very old, but he and Thal, his brother, had inherited the esteemed position upon the death of their father Bray, who had long held sway within his clan.) Zan spoke to Chul about the possibility of a new home. Elder though he was, Chul could be as excitable as any child. The proposal stimulated his appetite for adventure. He was a man who always had thrived on action, but had given up the wilder undertakings of his youth when the first baby came. Chul's short wife, Siraka-Finaka, had succeeded in tying the giant hand and foot, and he was always chafing and struggling against domesticity, for which he was actually rather poorly suited. When Zan first broke to him the idea of a migration of their entire people to this beautiful land, his jaw sagged and his eyes lit up. Then he thought of his wife, Siraka-Finaka, and frowned.

How should Chul persuade the chieftains of the desirability of such a move? He knew full well that he was slow of speech, and that whenever he did speak the listeners would smile and whisper to each other as though he were a fool—although any man would be a fool himself who dared to call Chul one! Who else could present the arguments persuasively? Dael would probably be silent as a stone; but on occasion Zan-Gah could prove an eloquent speaker. Had he not united the five clans to repel the wasp attackers when they were immersed in their ancient feud and were completely vulnerable to an alien assault? Zan would have to convince the men (the women need not be consulted) that this dangerous trek would be worth the effort. And Siraka-Finaka could do as she pleased.

▼ ▼ ▼

The chore of convincing the elders was not as difficult as they had expected. The hunt had failed, and the men of Ba-Coro were just returning from an almost fruitless search. Zan's group met them on the way. A council was soon held, and Zan prepared to make his arguments. Dael also, for his own reasons, was ready to back up his brother in council. Zan-Gah began with these words: "We have visited the land of the wasp people." There were exclamations of wonder. How had they escaped alive? "The wasp people are no more," Zan continued, and again there was uproar. Had these few travelers succeeded in killing the whole populous clan? What lies were they being told? Then Zan explained: "They fought among themselves in bloody war, but their final destruction was at the hands of a demon. Every one of them sickened and died, touched by the invisible fiend. By the time we arrived they were all dead, and how their bodies stank!" Zan did not mention Hurnoa's lone survival or her horrible murder. "The land is empty," Zan cried. "The demon has been expelled with fire, and the country is ours for the taking!"

Zan's listeners did not immediately understand why they should wish to take possession of the land. Dael, who seldom addressed a group, now spoke. In elaborate terms quite unlike his usual speech, he described the richness of the place: "Every time you put your hand in the water, you bring out a plump fish! Then you look across the lake and see deer on the far shore drinking and kissing their reflections! None of us need ever again be hungry!"

Dael described the fair flowering trees and swore that no one, seeing the country, would ever desire to live elsewhere. He was convincing. He did not speak of the hidden desire that motivated him—his mischievous longing to be closer to his old enemies, the Noi. In truth Dael cared nothing for the fruitful trees. He was already plotting revenge against his old enemies and tormentors.

Chul grunted an assent to Dael's persuasive words, and Zan added: "Why shouldn't our lives be easy and beautiful in a Beautiful Country? We would be happy and healthy, and even Aniah's old bones would cease to ache. It would be a land of healing!"

Aniah was a good listener and had held his silence, but now he spoke: "Every land seems fairer than the one you are in. What of the killing demon that dwells there? The wasp people were more numerous than we, and yet you say that they were completely overwhelmed. Those who rose so proudly in the morning were dead with the setting of the sun. Might we not be rushing to our death, and not our comfort? The journey alone could kill some of us! You and your brother are young and strong, Zan-Gah, but some of us are old. Others are babies in their mothers' arms. We will surely find new dangers and new enemies too. Why should we seek out those who hate us?"

Chul, who had a braying laugh, laughed now. "You have grown timid in your old age, Aniah. The killing devil is now gone, or we would not have survived to return home. Our bodies would at this moment lie stinking beside the corpses of the wasp men. Do not fear the journey, my friend. If you get tired walking, I will carry you on my back! Haw, haw!"

The men all laughed heartily at Chul's raspy guffaw, and at the thought of Aniah being carried on the giant's hairy back. Aniah laughed too. He and Chul were great friends, and often joked with each other. "I will be content to go, Chul," he said with a wink, "as long as I do not have to carry you!"

The men of Ba-Coro roared with mirth once again, but opinion was swaying in Zan's direction. Aniah preferred to present his views and then let others make the decision, and many more words were put forth, both for and against a move. Oin and Orah spoke up, confirming Dael's lavish description and boasting how they had fired the wasp men's houses.

Apparently, Zan, Chul, and the others had presented their project at a good time. These chiefs were weary of hunting without success. They were weary of struggling with their hostile, comfortless world. They wanted to see fruit trees in bloom and deer kissing the water! Some, indeed, were reluctant to move to a place where everyone had died, but the prosperity of the land tempted them. Thal, the father of the twins, came to Chul's aid and expressed his confidence in his sons and his "big brother." Everybody laughed again, and ended the council in a merry mood. A decision had been made.

The women had long been left alone, hungry for meat and hungry for their men. They were outraged to have waited so long for so little game, but they had been worried at the unusually lengthy absence of the hunters. Rejoicing and tender reunions greeted the men upon their return. Then there was amazement. No one had expected to be going anywhere; but they made no protest other than to grumble when Thal, Chul, Morda, and other elders told them to prepare for a long journey.

Many of the women felt slighted that they had not been invited to deliberations directly concerning their welfare, but they were hardly surprised to have been left out. They little expected to have a say, and knew that they would serve the men like beasts of burden, carrying and dragging water and supplies, while the men planned for their protection. However poor their land, they had dwelt on it for many generations. Their caves and hovels were their home and their safe shelter. Unwillingly the women did as they were told, gathering their possessions and waiting for favorable weather.

When, almost three months later, the time came to begin the journey, the Ba-Coro said farewell: to Nobla, the river that long had sustained them, to their sacred caverns, and to the tombs of the departed. Lissa-Na and her baby had died in one of the caves, and Dael visited their common grave the night before they left. Zan did so too—quietly and unknown to anybody.

Chul was elected the leader of the trek because he knew the way, and because his monstrous figure, seen in the forefront wielding a huge club, would tend to frighten off any enemies they might meet on the way. As the clans began their expedition, Chul intoned a hymn of rejoicing with his heavy bass voice, followed by a deep and dirge-like march in which all joined.

9 THE TREK

Weather is everything to those who travel the land, and the weather was good when the five clans of the Ba-Coro began their passage to the Beautiful Country. Autumn was approaching by the day of their departure, with its empty, bright blue skies and bracing gusts. Some foretold a speedy trip, but the progress turned out to be snail-slow. The women and especially the children were unused to travel, and the men were frequently obliged to go on hunting excursions to supply their needs and simply to give the weaker among them a chance to rest.

The elders began to worry. Winter was not so very far off, and the fair weather they had been enjoying could change at any time. And suddenly it did change. A whistling wind began to pursue them, carrying black clouds in their direction, while flocks of geese warped overhead, fleeing the blast with loud and raucous cries. A few drops were felt, then more, until the travelers were pelted and drenched by torrents. Half a dozen trees made a scanty shelter, and they hunched down, the men doing their best to protect the women and children. They could not build a fire, cold as they were, and could only sit, patiently enduring the icy downpour. Those who had animal skins wrapped themselves as best they might while rainwater dripped from their ragged beards. Zan and Pax were nestled together under Zan's large lion skin, more comfortable than most; and Rydl made no objection when Sparrow took shelter with him.

The storm got worse. An angry wind raved amidst the branches overhead, and below whole families huddled together for warmth. They sat without a word as lightning came and went, followed by claps of thunder that made the children cry. Perhaps these forlorn migrants would have suffered more if they were not used to it, but cold and rain were their usual fare. Still, people would get sick. Two days after the drenching a baby died, and Aniah had a rasping cough that boded no good. Several others were ill, and all were weary and wishing that they had never left the safety of their caves.

In time the weather turned fine again, but the air was crisp—colder than it had been earlier. A warming blaze became possible at last, and gave some relief. The men gathered around it, making plans, while the women were sent to gather fuel where they could find it. Then the clans moved on, treading the expanse of empty land to a rolling section where they would ascend to the brow of a hill and sink down, only to approach another rising and take it in their stride. The rains had left mires in the lower sections, which, for all the fair weather, were unpleasant to traverse. Whenever the band did cross these marshy places, they were slowed down and chilled. Carrion-devouring birds were seen circling overhead, but at last it was time to camp for the night, and a great new fire dispersed these creatures of prey.

The next morning, the clans awoke to an unusually thick fog that greatly limited their vision. The people were not inclined to move from their relative comfort when they could hardly see, and they began renewing their fires and warming themselves. However, the leaders, conferring together, resolved to press on, and goaded their clans to move. Every breath of wind reminded them that delay could be fatal.

But moving was dangerous too. Silence would be required. In the thick mist, careless chatter might alert unseen enemies and leave the group open to ambush; so a call for quiet was whispered from one to another. The men glanced around with unusual vigilance, clinging to their poison-tipped spears and readying themselves for anything that might spring at them. Every so often they were startled by the cry of a bird or animal they could not see.

The laborious, half-blind advance had not gone far when Chul, who was in the lead, motioned the train to stop. Just ahead, enveloped in fog and only faintly visible against the heavy, misty air, was the ponderous form of a mammoth. Its great domed skull, dark fur, and dangerous tusks would be seen close up, but at first it seemed almost as white as the surrounding vapor—a massive, monstrous blur. It turned out that its huge hooves were sunk in a morass of mud, and it was hardly able to move.

What luck! With a brusque hand signal and no word spoken, Chul alerted the numerous travelers. The babies were hushed and muffled as the women noiselessly drew back. At the same time, Chul waved some hunters forward with their envenomed spears.

The men knew what to do. Splitting into two groups, each band walked stealthily in single file to form a large ring around the great animal (a curl-tusked hill of hairy flesh), and at a signal threw their sharpened staves at their large target. The shrill elephant cry was dreadful as the men simultaneously struck. The mammoth struggled clumsily against the mire and the strange invaders, panic in its eyes. But it was doomed. The more the trapped beast strove, the more it slipped and sank. The thick hide protected it from an easy kill, but the powerful poison, entering through small wounds, did its work. The pathetic creature collapsed to its knees, flailing the ponderous trunk and screeching in terror. When it heavily lay down on its side, still wallowing, ropes were used to ensnare the hooves and trunk.

A few daring youths mounted atop the recumbent animal, among them Zan-Gah, who with grim efficiency stabbed at the animal's soft throat with repeated spear thrusts. When he hit an artery, the blood issued out in jets, covering most of Zan's body with the red shower and spilling onto the muddy bed beneath. The helpless animal thrashed and throbbed for a while, making strangled, snorting noises. Then its breath stopped and it was dead.

The hunters were silent at first, awed with their own accomplishment. Then, in the deep fog, and despite the danger of being overheard, a dull cheer of relief and rejoicing rose. It had been an easy kill, and here was meat enough for all the five clans! There would be no weary foraging for food for a while. Women and men began slashing the flesh with stone blades and axes, swarming over the hulk like hungry ants, or flocks of black-winged vultures, which, in a few hours, can strip a carcass clean.

Everybody was covered with blood, but they didn't seem to mind—and after a while a slow drizzle washed it away.

The cooking fires smoldered, but did not go out, and the aroma of roasted meat soon filled the air. All were happy. Strips of flesh were hung, and the tribes settled in again for the time required to dry them. The leaders chafed and murmured, anxious to get back on the move, but the people were already constructing makeshift huts on a low hill nearby and preparing for a stay. They were tired.

By dusk a congregation of wolves was heard gnashing and tearing at the carcass, for most of the flesh still remained, and its odor had reached their keen noses. Two wolves in particular drew the interest of the travelers, who, having gathered as much food as they could use, were watching the animals feast from a safe distance on the rising slope. The pair was fighting over a strip of muscle that one of them had torn off. Both clung to the same flank with their sharp fangs, tugging, snarling, and refusing to yield. The competition amused a number of the tribesmen, who noted the folly of fighting over a small amount when there was abundance for a hundred wolves and vultures! At last one of the animals let the meat loose, but only with the purpose of assailing his rival's throat. The witnesses above laughed loudly at this successful maneuver, and prepared to divert themselves with a struggle to the death.

Dael was not laughing, however. He was studying the combat with glowing eyes, drinking in the savagery as if he would acquire it for himself. Then, on a sudden impulse, he seized two spears and ran like a crazy man to attack the competing beasts. His friends called him to come back, but they were ignored. Dael threw one lance at the fiercer animal, piercing its chest and bringing it down with a yelp of pain. He attacked the other one too, forcing the second spear down its throat, as Zan-Gah had once killed the lioness. Dael then retrieved his weapons, panting for breath, and stood still with arms outstretched, a spear in each hand. His cry of triumph over the two dead animals was frightful to hear as he fairly shrieked to the sky. The spectators, stunned more by his wild cry than the deed itself, finally ran forward to protect him from the rest of the pack, for Dael was still in great danger; but the other wolves were so preoccupied with their greedy feed that they had ignored the entire episode and went on tearing and gnashing their fill. Their snarls would be heard throughout the night—and Dael was received like a hero.

Any part of a kill might be valuable. The slaughtered wolves were stripped of their pelts. Dael gave one of them to each of his Hru friends, Oin and Orah, who were delighted by the rich gifts. (They now were even more strongly drawn to their dominant friend and willing to follow his leadership.) The task of harvesting additional parts from the dead mammoth would be too time-consuming for people on the move, but someone wanted the tail, and Morda, the Hru chieftain, refused to leave the great tusks behind. It proved a long labor to cut these trophies from the carcass—which had begun to stink—but Morda owned hard stone blades, and slowly ground the tusks off with the help of Agrud, his long-suffering wife. As usual the women had been enlisted, carrying food, water, skins, and other necessities for long distances. Upon the eventual departure of the Ba-Coro from the site of their kill, the men marched ahead proudly, spears in hand.

Their wives trailed behind dragging their heavy loads on pole carriages, including the cumbersome tusks.

As the travelers moved over the bare, unpeopled land, they enjoyed a southern breeze for a while, but then it was driven out by a cold west wind. After the chilly day's trek, they took shelter by a stream in an area overgrown with brush—which contrasted with the rising and falling prairie. Suddenly Chul stopped to listen. His mouth always dropped open when he did, and he stared straight into empty space. He was hearing the shrill, whimpering sound of a small animal and he tried to locate its source. Dael happened to be nearby when, stepping into a cache of dry leaves, he was startled by a high-pitched yelp and a sharp pain on his shin. Dael reached down reflexively and discovered something warm and furry—two wolf cubs, one of which still had its small teeth in his leg.

These were probably the babies of one of the wolves he had killed. Dael picked a cub up with each hand by the scruff of the neck. They were weak with hunger and whining continuously. On the spot Dael adopted them and resolved to restore them. He brought them to vigorous health in a few days with water and prechewed bits of meat transferred from his mouth to theirs with careful fingers.

Zan and Pax noted with some curiosity and no little surprise the care and tenderness Dael lavished on the cubs. Zan's violent brother had always hated the species, dreaming sometimes at night in fitful sleep that whole wolf packs were surrounding and attacking him, while he tried in vain to fight them off. Horrid dreams! Besides, these were the offspring of animals he had recently slain simply for the fun and adventure of it. Yet Dael formed a sudden and strong attachment to them. They became his children and the focus of the little love that was still in him. Thereafter, wherever Dael went with his energetic and determined strides, the wolves would be behind. He would strike or even kick them when they displeased him, threatening to make a meal of them if meat should be in short supply; and yet they fawned on him and followed at his heels. By the time the clans reached their destination several months later, they were full-grown young wolves, as tame as their owner.

Dael trained them in toughness, tugging at toys in their mouths and fighting with them for their food. He sometimes amused himself by teaching his pets to howl. Sitting with them and holding one under each of his strong arms so that their heads were close together, he would begin to bark and keen in a way that drew a howling response from the animals. Then Dael, imitating them, would wail at the top of his lungs, *"arroo-roo-roo!"* causing them to howl even more. Perhaps it was the affect of their kinship, or maybe the noise just hurt their sensitive ears, but it was a strange concert. The three wailing together drew the laughter of all who saw them, and excited a good deal of admiration as well. Dael was already known for his fierceness and courage, and the company of his wild pets, forming something like a family, made him remarkable and respected by many, feared by some. Dael would leap with the animals, play with them, wrestle with them. And he began to seem like one of them. He enjoyed no one's company but theirs.

10 THE GREAT SPLIT

Possibly the most difficult part of the journey would be crossing the great split in the earth. It had been one thing for a small party of intrepid youths to traverse the harrowing, wind-swept expanse; it was quite another to expect women, children, and the aged to scamper fearlessly across the gulf as Rydl might! The depth of the gorge was absolutely terrifying, and the bridge built some years before by the wasp men was slender and unsteady.

Chul, who was a good parent, understood the need to prepare the children. Well before they came to the bridge he would lead a group of them around in single file, as a gigantic mother duck might walk its ducklings to water—to everybody's mirthful entertainment. It seemed to be a game, and the children enjoyed it, but it was really an exercise in trusting and following their leader. Yet when the time to cross the abyss arrived, Chul had to carry most of them in his arms or on his neck and shoulders, holding their urchin legs tightly in his grip. Rydl, that amazing acrobat, assisted, and even walked across on his hands to amuse the children and lessen their terror. Rydl was perhaps the only one of the entire group who was not intimidated by great heights.

There was another problem: Aniah was sick. He had become feeble with illness and extreme old age, and was so unsteady on his feet that Chul had to carry him on his back like one of the children—exactly as he had jokingly suggested some months before. Dael helped the women, who showed surprising courage and determination, while most of the men faced the ordeal with their usual bravado—each crossing accompanied by a chorus of cheers, laughter, and congratulations. How fierce Morda looked with a twisted elephant tusk over his shoulder! He made the crossing twice, risking his life to protect his prized possessions.

It was at this point that something unusual happened; Dael's thinking began to change. That intense and inexorable man, watching the fearless antics of his enemy Rydl, became aware that he admired him in spite of himself. For many weeks Dael had wished to get back at Rydl, and thought of little else. Once again he reflected on the way Rydl had trapped him in his snare—had lured and outsmarted him. And although he could still taste his humiliation, he had to admit to himself that Rydl was a clever and dexterous opponent, and no coward. He was forced to respect Rydl and, strangely, he almost started to like him. Maybe he would take his revenge, and maybe he wouldn't! Just now no private quarrel could be allowed to impede the difficult progress the Ba-Coro were making toward their new home. The elders simply would not tolerate it. Dael understood this and dropped for a time his former attitude of hostility, while still keeping his distance as he thought things over.

However, the volcanic nature of Dael's psyche led to another schism that resembled nothing so much as the deep split in the earth, which unnerved all who saw it. The divide, the new fatal gulf, was between Dael and his twin brother. It is difficult to say what caused it. There was no quarrel, only a striking difference in their personalities and outlooks leading to ever-increasing division and conflict. One might have supposed that they would enjoy each other's company, as they had during their younger years, now that they were reunited. But everything had changed. The brotherly friendship between them was gone.

Nor did it matter that they looked almost exactly the same—were mirror twins. The slight differences took on new importance. Zan still bore the scars of his battle with the lioness, whereas Dael's shoulders were unscarred. And Dael alone happened to be left-handed, a cause of wonder to all who noticed, and fear to some. The left hand was thought to be soiled and sinister, and Dael had been taught from his infancy to use his right. However, whenever he was upset about anything, he tended to revert to using the left, and Zan observed that he now regularly relied on it. He even seemed proud of his ability to use both hands and was determined to be different from his twin. Otherwise, the two were remarkably alike—physically.

So it was a strange fact that Dael was accounted much more handsome than Zan. What distinguished them? Was it something in their bearing or stance? Was it that Dael's intense eagle eyes conveyed conviction and authority, while Zan's were full of hesitancy and doubt? And why did Dael attract followers, each one of whom assumed a similar look of certainty, as if there were no other way to see the world but theirs?

It was true. Dael had acquired a following. Indeed his young men were fanatically devoted to him, almost slaves to his intractable will. And before long Zan-Gah had a troop of followers too, as large but less aggressive and warlike than his brother's. Since the return of Zan-Gah with his lost twin and the defeat of the wasp men in battle two years earlier, Zan had been an important young leader of the clan. But Dael had always resented his brother's ascendancy, and refused to follow in his shadow. Instead he went his own way, and soon a group, which included Oin and Orah, were trailing his loping, determined strides and responding to his peremptory commands.

Many of Zan's number were frightened by Dael's violence and recklessness; but other men were drawn to exactly these qualities. Those who loved one brother began to hate or jeer at the other, and in time as they walked to their western destination, the Ba-Coro tended to divide into two groups—one circling around Zan-Gah and the other around Dael. It happened so gradually and so naturally that for a while the division went unnoticed.

Dael was a born leader, yet Zan was also a leader in his way. It was Zan who had brought unity to the five clans and helped guide them to victory over the wasp people. Zan lacked Dael's dynamic personality, but he was respected for his wisdom, prudence, and ingenuity. Yet there was something terribly attractive about Dael's animal aggressiveness. In time it would appear how quickly Dael could lead his companions into danger, while Zan would prove as careful with his followers' lives as with his own. Every single one of the women favored Zan-Gah—a fact that Dael and his men quickly noticed and scoffed at. Zan's followers were called "women's men," and it was no compliment!

Where distress and sadness once could have been seen in Dael's eyes, there now dwelt a disturbing new arrogance and cruelty. Something new also crept into his speech. His tone was derisive, and filled with scorn for those with whom he disagreed. He could never pronounce "Zan-Gah" without giving "Gah" an undue, sarcastic emphasis. Even if others honored his brother, he had no intention of doing so. Rather, let Zan honor Dael—and beware of him! Zan observed his attractive brother with much more fear than admiration. Dael was like a force of nature now—a wild storm, a raging river, or a trapped animal that gnaws off its own leg. He was too dangerous to befriend, and too unyielding to advise or guide. Zan watched for any opportunity of reconciliation, but it was plain that Dael could not abide his twin or be swayed by him.

▼ ▼ ▼

More than once Dael had declared that he did not wish to have a twin, and started to do things to change his own appearance. He began by shaving his scalp and youthful beard. Zan would have the same wild curls as before, but Dael would not. Even more bizarre, Dael started to cut himself, as if he enjoyed the pain, enjoyed watching the blood trickle down his arms or legs. Sometimes he allowed his wolf-pups to lick the wounds, and when they scabbed over, he would pick at them and make them bleed anew— all the time absorbed and fascinated by his self-punishing injuries. No one but his closest friends noticed this private activity for a while, but once others did, Dael gave his self-laceration a special turn.

As if in parody of Zan-Gah's scars, which Zan had received from the lioness' claws, Dael began carving quite different swirling designs on himself. He decorated his thighs and stomach, and, with the help of friends, his shoulders, arms, and face. A dark dye was applied to make the marks striking and permanent. The result was a fierce new identity so different from his brother's that people who knew them both could hardly recognize them as twins. Soon Dael's friends, in imitation of their leader, shaved their heads and began to carve similar designs on their own bodies and on each other's. These physical alterations became their emblems, and the separation was complete: Dael's party was shaven and scarified, Zan's was not.

Some of the older men, and almost all of the women, recognized the inherent dangers of this schism. Aniah, feeble as he was, warned the tribes of the trouble they were making for themselves. Dael's father, Thal, spoke to Dael for a long time without result. Chul refused to join with either group, and deliberately walked between them. Yet he was well aware that it was Dael's party that fostered this dangerous separation, and his displeasure was apparent. Several of Dael's men began to direct their mockery at Chul, and Oin once attempted to trip him for the others' amusement; but Chul, without a word, kicked Oin in the backside and sent him sprawling.

When the tribes began their journey they had been a unified people; by the time they arrived in the new land they no longer were.

11 THE CRIMSON PEOPLE

The first open division came just after the tribes had crossed the chasm. That had been quickly done and was a success. There were no casualties. Dael declared that the bridge should be destroyed, and was ready to bring fire to it. "We will go in no direction but forward, so let us remove the means by which cowards might retreat!" Dael's partisans were ready to do his bidding as soon as a blaze could be started. But Zan, ever careful and prudent, protested loudly, and Chul scattered the smoldering twigs with his foot. Morda and several others agreed with Dael, and gave their reasons, but Zan's more numerous supporters prevailed and the Ba-Coro moved on, the elders leading the way. The two contending groups followed them, and the women brought up the rear with their baggage. The wasting Aniah still had to be carried, and Chul, his friend, patiently bore the burden.

The earth was gradually becoming red as they approached the magnificent land of the red rocks. Zan and Rydl loved that country. The two had been happy when they lived there, and familiar sights brought back pleasant memories of the independent life they had enjoyed. Zan especially felt the renewed pleasure of adventure, and looked once again at the skull-like forms in the rocky walls flanking them. They revisited the cave dugout that had been their home—the "mouth" of the skull. Rydl reminded Zan of the time they had snatched partridges from a wildcat, and laughed. Zan still remembered the good dinner, and Rydl recalled to himself how, as a lost little boy, he had first begun to love and trust Zan-Gah. Entering the cool interior, they saw the mystical carved sign etched in the wall, and noticed that the store of grain beneath it was gone. Someone else had been there.

This was not a heavily populated area. Zan had passed through it four times without seeing a single soul, although he had occasionally noticed footprints in the reddish dust and knew that it must be occupied, or at least visited. The land, strewn with boulders great and small, provided many hiding places in the jagged shadows, dugouts, and collapsed cliffs. Zan loved and marveled at the sight of them, but now he perceived how dangerous they might be. At that moment, the Ba-Coro were threading their way through the maze of rocks. When the meandering reddish creek offered refreshment, everybody paused to rest.

Meanwhile a few men, Zan among them, kept a vigilant watch. Aniah, sick as he was, had alerted Chul to the danger of ambush, and Chul had passed the message of caution to others. Sharp-eyed Pax also addressed the danger, and was the first to notice that some of the red rocks seemed to be moving. It was not her imagination! Pax's hunting sensibilities were so highly trained that the tiniest motion was visible to her. *"Oh ah ah! Oh ah ah!"*

she cried shrilly at the top of her voice, causing the men nearby to start.

There was no mistaking her alarm! Everybody looked up. Everybody looked around. But nobody saw anything unusual, and although they listened intently, heard nothing but the scream of a bird. "They are there! They are there!" she cried, pointing to the field of boulders that lay before them. And suddenly they *were* there, rising from the ground and flinging their strange weapons at Dael's party, which had advanced somewhat farther than the others. The attackers employed unusual sharpened discs, which sailed through the air and sliced whatever they struck.

No one ever had seen anything like these weapons, or the men who wielded them. The warriors were clean-shaven and virtually naked, and their bodies were entirely reddened from the top of their skulls to the base of their feet with crimson paint, so that crouched down they looked exactly like the red boulders that filled the valley, or the vivid earth from which the paint was made. They had seen the approaching strangers and rolled themselves into human balls to disguise themselves as stones.

It was a very successful camouflage. Had they remained absolutely still, the entire population of the Ba-Coro could have passed a few feet from enemies without even noticing their presence—leaving themselves absolutely vulnerable to a surprise assault. As it was, the red men seemed to have sprung from the earth. It was as if the stones themselves had come to life to attack them.

Oin was wounded. A disc had sliced his shoulder in the fleshy part, and he was crying and sobbing. It was his first wound. His brother Orah was crying too, as much as if he also had been gashed. Meanwhile, Dael's party responded to the attack with a volley of sling-flung stones, and then rushed the new foe with their spears. Dael was absolutely fearless in battle, and his men, taking strength and courage from their leader, imitated his ferocity. Dael was also pitiless, and with the help of his followers, left several bloodied red corpses to dry in the sun. The red men fled and hid, and the Ba-Coro marched on, ready for any further incursions.

There were no other incidents, however. Probably the crimson men, having lost the element of surprise, and knowing that they were well outnumbered, realized that further attacks would be unsuccessful. But Zan's people did not know this, and had to be ready to repel further assaults. These never came; but now every red boulder was a little more frightening and suspect than it had been before.

Zan learned much later that both men and women of this tribe shaved their heads and bodies smooth with their sharpest blades, and painted themselves with the ubiquitous crimson pigment. Their scanty clothing, weapons, and ornaments, and even their teeth, were reddened. This was their constant wear, and they thought it beautiful. To be without it was shameful in their eyes, like being naked.

The color rendered them almost invisible to potential enemies; neither Zan nor anyone else had known of their existence because they were so hard to see. Their red hue distinguished and unified them as a people, and it proved an effective tactic of war. But it was also a religious expression. Becoming like earth and rocks was viewed as an act of worship and a token of respect for the Mother. They were the red earth's children, had reddish priests, and indeed their entire lives were shaped by the unusual character and color of the land they lived in.

▼ ▼ ▼

That night there was a council among the Ba-Coro. Many concerns had to be addressed, chief among them security. A plan of guard was settled, and Pax was thanked for her watchfulness—but not appointed. There were minor concerns needing attention as well as major ones. Even on the trail, marriages had to be arranged and babies were being born. Intertribal mating had gone far in uniting the five separate clans that had once been at each other's throats, but the Hru still tended to hold apart, and now the new division between Dael's people and the others threatened to destroy the progress they had made in coming together. Conflict was just beneath the surface, and this became a topic of urgent discussion.

Aniah, now close to eighty winters old, meant to speak. His age and sickness showed. He could not go hunting any more, and was often seen dozing where he sat. So feeble that he was hardly able to stand, Aniah yet maintained his dignity and authority, which had been based on the love of his people more than fear or force. His wisdom and experience were still valued, and he addressed the meeting despite his illness, warning of the dangers of the growing disunity. He, as many of the older tribesmen, knew enough of feuds to remember how one act of hostility could lead to many others. Much of Aniah's life had been spent dealing with a recurrent cycle of hatred, vengeance, and unceasing tribal conflict.

The men agreed, after an acrimonious argument, not to play or joke with poisoned spears. Dael, who was most apt to offend in this way, promised to refrain, and made his men promise too. Dael would keep his word; for all his unsettled faults, that could be counted upon. As it happened, the Ba-Coro did not much like the poison formerly favored by the wasp people. Accidents frequently happened, often self-inflicted, and the men had already begun to avoid using it.

Aniah had long meditated on Dael's afflictions, and realized that he could not quell the fire that burnt inside of him. But he spoke to Dael—not for the first time—as a father would to his son: "The time will come that you will leave us and go far away, for you have that within you which will not let you be happy with any people. You must seek your destiny alone, and in time you will." Then the old man addressed the chiefs once more with glittering eyes, charging them to protect their friendship and unity, which was the backbone of their strength. He was trembling and short of breath and could not speak for very long. It was to be Aniah's last advice to the Ba-Coro, well remembered by those who loved him.

Dael, not to be restrained by Aniah's admonition, now demanded the speaker's staff. He had scarcely contained his rage, but now it came forth in an unexpected way. Pointing at Zan-Gah with the rod, and shaking it at him the entire time he was speaking, he loudly asserted that his twin had been to blame for the attack of the red men.

"I wanted to burn the bridge behind us to protect our rear! These painted people could have been prevented from following us! Now Oin is wounded, and we are lucky it is no worse!" (Oin could be heard whimpering a short distance away.)

Dael made no sense to thoughtful people. The red men had been ahead, not behind, and it seemed extremely unlikely (although not impossible) that they had crossed the bridge behind the Ba-Coro and somehow gotten to the red rocks before them for an ambush. Besides, their crimson camouflage was not a technique quickly improvised. Probably, it was a long-standing method employed by people who had always lived within this red land—and not on the other side of the chasm where natural colors were more subdued. Nevertheless Dael's friends applauded his speech with the pounding of spears and loud grunts of assent, and were not soon quieted.

Dael continued when it became possible: "It is your fault, Zan-*Gah!*" he cried, still shaking the rod. "Yours and that great hulk of yours who kicks out fires. These red men came at us because we failed to destroy the bridge!" Dael was extremely angry, and Zan made no reply. He did not wish to quarrel with his own brother before the entire council. It would only make things worse. How could he hope to deal with the poisonous mixture of grief and fury that swayed and misshaped Dael's thoughts? His eyes fell from Dael's eyes to his torso. For some reason Dael's tattooed chest was much more hairy than his own. Zan had to confront the fact that he no longer liked his twin brother. He loved him but he did not like him. He pitied him, feared him, and feared for him.

Dael turned to Chul, pointing at him as the cause of the attack because he had preserved the bridge, and moreover accusing him of being laggard in the fight. Chul received the rebuke with a shrug. He had been carrying Aniah at the time of the attack, and was actually some distance away. Chul said not a word. He just pointed to the scar on his leg. Every one of the older men remembered how Chul had once brought a bloody battle to a victorious conclusion with a spear stuck in his thigh the whole time. This was the remains of that injury. Many could still hear Chul's dreadful cry of war, and well recalled the fierceness with which he had led the attack despite the wound.

Chul did not even answer the other charge concerning the bridge. He only scoffed that Dael seemed not to know his front from his behind. The men laughed at this, and several women, listening from the sidelines, tittered audibly. Dael's pride was hurt and his anger was greater than ever.

Dael threw down the speaker's rod furiously. He had no more to say. The meeting, long afterwards remembered as "the council of blame," came to an end. Feelings were more intense than they had been in several years, and the division was deeper than before. Aniah would have said a few more words of conciliation, but he was so weakened by his exertions that he was physically incapable of doing so.

A few days later the aged and revered chieftain died. For a brief time the rival factions forgot their quarrels as universal respect was paid to a great leader. A huge barrow was amassed over his remains, directly under the majestic stone arch, which would usher the Ba-Coro into the Beautiful Country.

12 THE BEAUTIFUL COUNTRY

It was late winter when the Ba-Coro arrived at the land Zan called Beautiful, and although it was not very cold, a fresh, untouched snow was on the ground and delicately laced the trees. Nobody seemed to notice the loveliness of the newly whitened landscape; snow was cold to those who walked on it, not beautiful.

Yet the journey was not as difficult as it might have been. When one knows where one is going it is easier, even if not a step is saved. The people, always sensitive to the need for water, gathered around the lake facing the waterfall. The cascade, which had been frozen into a solid stream, was beginning to melt, and was dripping, rather than running with its usual thunderous fall. The lake was still frozen, but the shell of ice was too thin to walk on.

It was difficult to build fires because of the moisture everywhere, but fortunately a few women had preserved dry tinder for just such situations. As they labored to kindle it, the men were free to seek materials and build shelters. Here Rydl, who knew something of the wasp men's abodes, showed the cave dwellers how to weave slender branches around saplings to construct rudimentary houses. Later they would smear them with mud to seal them from the chilling winds, or perhaps some tar could be found. That is what the wasp people used—and what had burned so brightly when their nests were torched. The next night it snowed again, but the people were warm in their huts by then. Rydl did not mind that Sparrow stayed with him in the hut they built together.

A week later most of the snow had melted and was streaming in rivulets to the little brooks that ran into the lake. The ice on the lake was gone except for the distant shady side of it, near where the waterfall was. The cascade was thawing too, and occasionally giant spears of ice came crashing down.

Life was returning to the land. There might be reverses in the weather, but spring was visibly arriving. The flinty skies of winter came less and less to freeze the blood, and soon fled from the southern breezes. A more genial climate made itself at home. Zan and Pax, happy with their new surroundings, had their own hut and woke up smiling each day. Dael had a shelter too, more open than theirs and a distance away. He still avoided Zan and Pax, keeping company with his own group and giving commands to his subordinates to build for him. There were two groups of huts now, not one.

The transformation that spring brought was lovely to see, and lifted everyone's spirits. As the snow gradually retreated, the reluctant buds began to show themselves, followed by glowing and flamboyant blossoms that ringed and colored the glistening water. The island in the middle of the lake came to life too. Its white birch trees were still there, only taller, with a few dead trees keeping company with the living. Every morning they saw the same doe drinking or grazing on the lake's far side, and the broad-winged egrets cast their reflections when they flew low over the still water's surface. Who could fail to rejoice at the sight of unfamiliar, brightly colored birds and the sweet and varied sounds of their mating calls?

The Ba-Coro flourished in their enchanting new home. Babies were being born. Food was plentiful. And the men began to explore the new area hopefully. It appeared that most of their good fortune was yet to come. Best of all, the troublesome division seemed to be healing. People were too dependent on each other for the breach to last for very long, and Dael contemplated whether he should mend his relationship with "the wasp-child," as he called Rydl. Dael did not want to defeat his enemy in a fight. He already knew that he was the stronger man. No, he wanted to humiliate Rydl as Rydl had humiliated him. He waited for his chance, but Rydl was too clever for him. Dael found himself watching and studying him.

Rydl was always busy with his projects and inventions. It was one of his quirks (which Dael found unforgivably effeminate) that Rydl was artful about his appearance. Rydl learned to sew smaller skins together with a needle of bone and fibers of animal ligament for thread, attractively patching differently colored pelts. He was by far the best dressed of the Ba-Coro, tailoring and decorating his garments much more than was common among them. Dael found his primping disgusting.

However, Dael's feelings were quite different when Rydl tried combining the virtues of the spear and the sling. Weapons interested Dael, and his fancy enemy was engaged in improving them. Rydl had reasoned that if a sling could make a rock go faster and farther, might it not increase the speed and power of a spear's thrust? After many attempts Rydl had given up on the sling. It was too supple and could not be controlled. But he devised a spear-thrower of wood that used the same principle as the rock-thrower. In effect it lengthened the throwing arm, just as a sling did. It was more rigid than the sling, and it worked amazingly well. Dael, who often observed Rydl from a distance, was impressed. He saw, as Rydl practiced, that his spear sailed considerably farther than his own did; and when it hit the target, it penetrated much more forcefully. After only a short time Dael swallowed his pride and asked Rydl to show him how it worked, and Rydl did. The spear, lighter and slenderer than usual, was laid on a short grooved staff with a tooth-hook to hold it in place; then the spear was flung with the staff, not directly by hand. And how it flew! Dael immediately adopted Rydl's invention, and soon all the men were using it. Now they were better armed than ever. Thereafter Dael treated Rydl with some respect, although it might be a long time before they could feel friendship for each other.

Rydl had other problems. He noticed how sad Sparrow had lately become in his presence, and how she tended to follow him with her eyes when she thought he was not looking. She seemed to be expecting something that did not come, and it weighed on her heavily. The speaking lessons became more somber and businesslike. They did not sing or laugh together as before.

"Why don't you marry that poor girl who loves you?" Chul asked him without ceremony one day. "You need a wife, and anyone can see that she is willing." Rydl responded with a thoughtful and quizzical smile but said nothing.

Sparrow always tried to please Rydl by speaking, but she could only make uncouth sounds for all her efforts, except when she sang very softly to herself. Then she would try to shape the words Rydl had taught her:

The w-w-wolves h-h-howl,
The b-b-birds s-s-sing,
And Sp-Sp-Sp-Sparrow sp-speaks her n-n-n-name.

Rydl overheard one morning and assured her that she was making fine progress. She looked deeply and sadly into his eyes and tried desperately to say something without singing it. On occasion Rydl touched her face, mouth, and even her tongue in an attempt to aid her; and now Rydl came very close, hoping to help stabilize her speech. With painful difficulty Sparrow now spoke her first sentence: "I l-l-l-love you R-R-Rydl."

Rydl almost jumped when he heard these broken words, surprised to hear anything coherent, but especially startled to hear *that*! It was plain that Rydl did not return her strong affection. Sparrow blushed at her words, and then turned deathly pale, looking directly in Rydl's eyes and waiting for a reply. None came. Rydl would have her believe that he did not quite hear her, and attempted to continue the lesson as if nothing remarkable had been said. But it *had* been said, and Sparrow, unable to endure his silence, ran away.

The lessons stopped after that. From then on Sparrow looked coldly at Rydl, or turned away when he passed. She no longer kept him company. Rydl was saddened, but he was sadder when Sparrow started to give Dael marked attentions in his presence. She slept very near Dael's hut now, and sometimes brought him food and gifts. She did him small services, and walked beside him whenever she could. And worse, Dael encouraged her with friendly looks and touches, knowing well how Rydl would take it. Dael had decided to win her heart, and that could be his revenge on Rydl. For once Dael would win, he thought with satisfaction. For once Dael would get the best of "the wasp-child."

Dael contemplated handing Sparrow over to Oin, but Sparrow herself was not as bashful and shamefaced as Oin was in the presence of females. Dael did not want her for himself, and was only laughing at her and Rydl. Sparrow certainly was not interested in Oin! She detested both him and his brother who had so often jeered at her.

▼ ▼ ▼

Those two wanted to go hunting for something they were not afraid of, and chose to bring down the doe that frequently appeared on the far side of the lake. Dael, who was always restless for action, went along, and for some reason Pax decided to quietly follow them from a distance. Zan had been lazing around, and had nothing better to do than to keep her company. Pax warned him to avoid being observed.

Dael's former description of deer kissing their reflections on the water was apt. The gentle animal they hunted was always to be seen, morning and evening, wading into the shallower water and peacefully drinking, so that her face actually met and seemed to kiss its reflection. Apparently she did not fear the distant tribesmen, nor suspect that they might come to kill her.

Dael and his friends were not good hunters. Accustomed to pushing ahead without taking thought, they had little mastery of the delicate art of stalking game. At first they loudly crashed their way through the trees, but as they approached their quarry they made an effort to move very carefully and quietly. They were soon within striking distance of the deer, with Pax and Zan closer behind than they realized. Dael had fashioned and learned to use the new spear-throwing device, and was an excellent marksman; but low-hanging branches stood in the way of the spear's path, and he had to maneuver around to get a clear throw. Oin and Orah were following him, evidently content to let their leader have the first strike.

They still had no idea that Pax and Zan were nearby, and all three hunters readied their flint-tipped weapons. When a sharply snapping sound alerted the doe, however, Dael thought Orah had carelessly stepped on a dry twig. The deer raised its head suddenly, ears outspread and senses alert, charged into the thicket, and was gone. Dael kicked Orah in the buttocks with his bare foot, and the three turned to go back. Orah did not even ask why he had been kicked, taking it for an expression of Dael's bad temper. Zan and Pax hid themselves, and the three spear bearers walked right past without seeing them.

"Why did you make that noise, Pax?" Zan inquired after the hunters had gone some distance. "You knew that snapping a stick would frighten the doe away."

"We do not need meat right now," she said almost angrily. Zan looked at her with surprise and she added: "I see that doe every morning when we wake up, and I like looking at her." And she marched ahead without waiting for an answer. From behind Zan regarded her with amazement and admiration. "What a strange and wonderful woman I have married," he thought to himself. He should have said as much to her, but it was his nature—and his failing—to be silent.

Meanwhile, Dael and his companions were diverted by a surprising sight. It was beginning to get dark, and the fires of the Ba-Coro were plainly visible across the lake. But on their own side, only a little distance inland, a single campfire blazed. Whose was it? Could it be the red men? Dael slowly ventured in its direction, Oin and Orah right behind him. Zan and Pax took this as an opportunity to slip past them and return to their camp. Only the next morning did the other three get back—and there was blood on Dael's spear.

13 THE FIRE-MOUNTAIN

Dael had not discovered a camp of the red men as he supposed at first. When he saw the beds of the men of Noi arranged around their campfire, he could not restrain himself. He knew them by their dress and ornaments, and the sight was maddening. He thought he recognized two as his former tormentors, and without waiting for his companions he rushed at them and slew them before they could get up, one with his spear and the other with a large rock that was at hand. There were two more who, alarmed by the sudden assault and unsure of the number of their attackers, fled into the forest and were seen no more.

On returning, Dael did not mention the bloody encounter to anyone, but his companions did, enthusiastically enlarging on Dael's courage and ferocity. The entire camp was soon talking of a likely battle. Older warriors like Morda and Chul seemed worried and spoke of the need for defenses and sentinels. The women began looking about them for possible danger, and although the children still ran and played, their mothers kept them closer than usual.

For many days nothing happened, and people began to forget about the danger, but after a month or more had passed, a large group of fires was seen reflecting on the far side of the lake. Whole families of the Noi were visible across the water, indicating that war had not been their purpose in coming. It appeared, rather, that the Noi also had decided they would prefer to live in this fruitful region instead of the desert, and had made a migration similar to that of the Ba-Coro.

Each group was aware of the other and, because blood had unluckily been spilled, both feared a possible war. But war did not come. The new arrivals were busy building, and each group seemed content to let the other strike first—except for Dael, who was grimly pleased to have the Noi within his reach and would gladly have attacked the new settlers single-handed. His friends restrained him, however, and he decided to wait for the right moment.

▼ ▼ ▼

It was not a good time for Dael. The sight of Noi warriors brought back a flood of painful memories, and the world almost turned black before his eyes. His darkest thoughts revived and every inward wound was made fresh. During the day he was listless and dreamy, but as night approached he seemed to come to life like a nocturnal animal, his face agitated by his intense ruminations. When he finally slept he seemed even more distressed, troubled as he was by vivid and ghastly dreams. His groaning disturbed his fellows, and Zan, who had been watching Dael's deterioration with dismay, pondered what he could do to calm him. He suspected that Dael wanted to die, and a man with this desire is dangerous to everybody, not just himself.

One night Zan tried to talk to his brother, although they were not on good terms and rarely communicated. Dael surprised him by listening, but would say nothing himself. He only clenched his teeth and stared furiously into the empty air. Zan spoke of anything he could think of, hoping to get his brother to open up to him. He touched on subjects of hunting, of their happy childhood, even of Dael's enemies and the threatening war—all in vain.

After these failed attempts, Zan took a perilous step. He gently broached the subject of Dael's dead wife, Lissa-Na. Dael started at the sound of her name. His expression was of one who might well burst into flame, so intense and contradictory were his passions. How could Zan know that it was often of her that Dael dreamed; that even as he was savoring in sleep the sweetness of her love and those tender explorations that lips and fingers make, he would be attacked and torn by his enemies with their furious and horrifying faces—the Noi, who were her people and her blood? He dreamed of his lost baby covered with blood, and was visited by troops of fragmented, frightening memories that were half real and half ghost.

Dael could scarcely bear to hear Lissa's name spoken. He cut Zan off sharply, crying to him to be silent and never, never to speak of her. But after a short period he began to talk softly about her himself; and as he did he roughly jostled his two pets who, seeming to understand, pressed closer to their master and listened to his voice.

"In my worst moments then, when I was their captive, she came to me in the dark of night, bringing me food and whispering a few words to comfort my misery. You know, Zan, she had a low and gentle voice. One could have loved her for her voice alone, but that was the least of her virtues. Her beauty was hardly of this world. Do you remember how much everybody admired her and tried to imitate her? She was like a goddess! And she was unaffected by all the eyes that followed her, as though she were completely unaware—or else thought all that admiration was her due and not to be noticed." Zan quietly agreed although deeply moved by his memories. He had loved her before Dael, and wanted her when Dael had been too sick to want anybody.

"Her wisdom," Dael continued, staring straight ahead, "was as great and noble as her beauty. She knew the secrets of the earth to heal the ill and wounded. And she could see into your heart, Zan, detecting thoughts and feelings you hardly knew you had—isn't that so Zan?"

Zan was stirred, and a tear might have been seen forming in his eye if it had not been so dark. "Yes, Dael," he said because he had to say something. He remembered her as if she were standing in front of them. "She nursed me to health after I had almost died in the desert. Suddenly I found myself a patient in her quiet cave. She was bending over me with her gorgeous hair falling on my face and shoulders. It would be difficult not to... admire her, to...love...her."

It was Dael's turn to listen, but in his illness he was subject to violent changes of mood, and now he altered abruptly for the worse: "Yes, you pig, you wanted her. I knew it then. Did you think I couldn't see your lovesick eyes searching her out—oh yes, even after we were joined in marriage? Even after you were coupled with your own man-bride? Do you think that I am blind, or was ever ignorant of your womanish infatuation?" The fire illuminated one side of Dael's face, lending it a frightening aspect while the other side was black as night.

Zan could deny nothing of what Dael said, and stated in honest terms that he had loved Lissa-Na as much as honor allowed. He did not admit that he had burned with love for her, but Dael knew he had.

"And yet you let me take her from you—you the great lion killer Zan-*Gaaah!*"

"I don't know why Lissa chose you over me," Zan said. Her vision floated before him. "I used to think that you were almost worthy of her, but I begin to change my mind."

"I told you before and I tell you again: Do not ever dare to speak her name to me, or who knows what I might do? Leave me. Leave me and don't trouble me any more."

There could be no profit in continuing the conversation once it had taken this unpleasant direction. Zan rose, turned sharply, and left. He did not realize that Pax, who happened to be busy nearby, had overheard most of what was said—had heard her husband praise Lissa-Na and confess that he loved her. That was bad luck, and there was more to come; but what Zan said was no more than what she already knew.

▼ ▼ ▼

The next morning Zan approached Dael as if nothing had happened the night before. He had been looking for a chore that would distract his brother from his grief, and carry him away from the Noi before something dreadful happened. Rydl had suggested a project for which a good deal of help would be required.

"We need tar, Dael," Zan announced. "It is a better sealer than mud, and will help keep the cold out of our shelters this winter. Rydl thinks he knows where it can be found—in the direction of the midday sun behind some of these hills." Dael looked over his shoulder toward the sun and squinted. With one foot he stirred the wolves sleeping nestled against him, rose, called to Oin, Orah, and some other friends, grabbed his weapons, and strode off with Zan and Rydl.

▼ ▼ ▼

That same day Pax was looking for the polished green stone Lissa-Na had given her during the time they were still friends. Why she was searching so eagerly for Lissa's gift the morning after she overheard Zan's confession she probably could not have said. She was unable to find it, but she did uncover something that confirmed all of her jealous fears. It was a thick strand of Lissa's hair, which had been woven into a compact braid. Pax recognized it instantly by its color, and knew it was Zan's private possession. Zan kept it still...because he loved her still! What other explanation was there?

Angry tears formed in her eyes in spite of her attempts to control them. Pax laid the memento on Zan's bedding where he could not miss it, took up her spear and a few possessions, brushed the water from her cheeks, and walked into the woods in the direction opposite to her husband's. She was resolved that she would not be there when he came back.

▼ ▼ ▼

Zan's party had headed south, where the land was much different from the leafy area in which they lived. After a few miles, the ground began to soften and the muddy earth started to bubble, giving off an offensive, sulfurous odor. It was a scary, mysterious place. The trees were hung with long strands of moss, nurtured by pools of steaming water of an unnatural blue-green iridescence. Orah foolishly put his toe in one and burned himself, and Dael, who never laughed but to mock, gave out a guffaw. Orah laughed too while he grimaced with pain.

Later they noticed that the plants and trees, which all sloped in the same direction, were sprinkled with gray dust and seemed less and less healthy. Even the ground had become coated with ashes when finally, toward the end of the day, they discovered the cause of these peculiar changes looming before them. They saw it and heard it too, for a low, angry rumble had been audible from some distance. The group looked around apprehensively.

Between the two mountains on either side of the travelers was a third at some distance, shrouded in a smoky mist and only half visible from where they stood.

All three were capped with snow, except that the central one, open at the top, sent up a column of rolling smoke. Bursts of fire and showers of hot sparks exploded from its ragged peak, followed moments later by loud growling noises. At each eruption the ground shook. The mountain's pure shape rose upward in even, symmetrical arcs that were both simple and sublime, while the fountain of fire at the apex challenged and polluted the sky.

The entire band was stunned by the vision before them, but Dael was overwhelmed, as if in the mountain of fire he had discovered his personal god. To him it was a living giant whose angry thunder seemed to speak a language he might hope to understand.

The immense peak seemed close, though it was whole days away; and the group was separated from it by a stark, lifeless landscape. There, jagged, deeply fissured rocks hissed gases and emitted foul-smelling steam—an unwholesome, impassable expanse. Dael slowly ventured as close as he dared, gazing at the cauldron of fire in rapt wonder, his hands outspread. His companions watched him as well as the volcano, aware that a mighty turmoil was churning within their friend, and followed him as he slowly went forward.

The day was coming to an end and the sun was about to set behind the mountain's smoke. The vivid and unnatural red disc peered through the density of the cloud—tolerable to the human eye but intolerable to the spirit. All of the men were frightened and unnerved; only Dael seemed to welcome what he saw. He sat down with his legs crossed, facing the mountain in rapture. Oin,

Orah, and his pets sat on either side of him. Zan, Rydl, and some others, not entirely aware of Dael's fixation, decided to look around for tar as was their original purpose, but because night was approaching they soon returned and made a camp nearby.

Meanwhile Dael was regarding the bursts of fire with fascination, reverence, and awe. As the fire mountain roared and rumbled he gave himself over to the display and to the earth shuddering beneath him. These strangely duplicated the convulsion within him, mirroring his own volcanic inner turmoil—smoking, burning, exploding. With the coming of darkness the mountain itself was gradually less visible, while the fire and sparks belching from it presented a spectacular, mind-arresting show.

Dael remained there without moving, and perhaps his rapture was contagious, for his men stayed beside him, watching in awe both the volcano and their transformed leader. Soon only the fiery cataclysm was visible against the night sky. A burst of yellow sparks thrown from the molten heart of the mountain stood out against the blue-black sky, reflecting its brilliance in the fixed eyes of the watchers, while a glowing vein of lava trickled like blood down the smooth slope.

Zan knew too well the expression on Dael's face. His brother's teeth were clenched and his gleaming eyes rolled and darted with each jet of fire, as if a theater of battle flashed before him; or else as one who intensely regards something invisible to ordinary men. Zan urged Dael to come away, and tried without success to make him rise. At that very moment an explosion shattered one side of the rim, vomiting fire and lighting the sky, so that all of the viewers froze in shock and dread. Dael alone was exultant, shouting in a rapture of joy and triumph: "The god pours forth fire! Fall down and worship!" And he fell on his hands and knees, touching the trembling ground with his scarred forehead. Nothing Zan could do would make him get up, and Dael's companions, who had also cast themselves down, were no help. Dael's mysterious delirium was sacred to his fellows, who already held his iron temperament in awe.

In dismay Zan left their presence to confer with Rydl and another lad and to enlist their aid. From a distance he could hear Dael scream, "Now arise! The heart of the fire-mountain bursts!" Zan turned to look, while Dael, who was standing once again, began to address the grisly mountain and its beckoning sparks. Then he seemed to turn toward Zan. His eyes were rolling wildly in his head, and suddenly his legs twisted and collapsed. Dael's mouth was still open and his eyes were searching for the back of his head as he fell in a swoon and came crashing to the earth. Rushing to him, Zan could do nothing but try to pillow his head. When the dawn approached hours later, Oin and Orah were weeping over their fallen comrade as if he were dead.

Even Zan feared that Dael had expired, overcome by the violence of his own emotions or fatally injured by his fall; but after a time Dael revived and stood up as though nothing unusual had occurred, or as if he were awakening from a deep, restful slumber. He was unhurt, and as was the case with the volcano itself, much calmer than he had been the night before.

Everyone looked at him with wonder and fear. Dael actually seemed taller than he had been, and had a new serene bearing and peaceful expression. He moved slowly now and spoke softly, even gently, when spoken to. But his companions were anything but serene. They looked on him as one arisen from the dead—as one who had gone to the lower world to converse with departed spirits and could deliver their messages. All wished to know what he had seen and heard. Oin and Orah asked if he had spoken with their mother who had died two years earlier. Dael made no reply except to nod absently. He seemed to have forgotten all about the volcano. Zan asked him if he were recovered and Dael smiled—*smiled!*—and said that he was.

But in the afternoon, when the volcano resumed its unruly and turbulent activity and spoke again with its voice of thunder, Dael's fixation returned. For long hours he sat before the mountain in rapture, responding to its every outburst with an intense, joyful identification. Once again he seemed to be in communion with spirits or invisible things, while his companions looked on with a new increased reverence. Only Zan and Rydl continued to see Dael as disturbed and sick. The others regarded him as a prophet, and began to call him Dael-Destan—Dael the Seer.

Late that night Dael fainted again.

14 THE BRAID OF HAIR

Zan could not understand what was happening. The roiling volcano, which was only an interesting sight to him, became the center of Dael's world, his all in all, and his holy of holies. It was impossible to get Dael away from the mesmerizing sight. He clung to the point of observation he had chosen for himself as if it were a temple and the whole explanation of his existence lay in the immense blazing peak and its shattering explosions. He would sit transfixed before the altar of the fire-mountain as though all he looked for in the world were there on the burning summit. His lips would move in a murmuring prayer barely audible to his companions, but deeply felt: "Great and terrible fire, you are my parent and my god! You spit in the face of the sky, and so do I! You are defiant and so am I! Your power is my power! I give myself to you and worship you!"

Zan caught enough of his brother's passionate words to be filled with dread for him. It was soon afterwards that Dael fainted the second time, and in the morning he awoke in an unnaturally calm state as before. Once again the activity of the volcano had subsided, putting forth only its calmer stream of white vapor, which was its usual condition.

Dael's fit had passed and he began to think of other things. Zan got his brother to eat something for the first time since well before they had discovered the mountain, and suggested that they go home. He wondered aloud if their presence might be needed now that the Noi had settled across the lake. Dael fairly leapt at his words as if Zan had touched him with something hot. It was becoming clear that Dael was torn between two separate obsessions. When the volcano was active Dael could think of nothing else, but as soon as Zan reminded him of the Noi, all of his emotions were transferred to his old enemies and his desire for their destruction. One passion drove out the other; there was no room for both. Zan decided that if he were to get his brother home he would have to encourage the second of these fixations for a time. "We must help guard our people," he insinuated to Dael, who suddenly was all eagerness to go.

When the group got back to their camp the elders were talking together with anxious faces. Across the lake were an alien people, but were they to be feared or possibly welcomed? It was hard to tell, and a mistake could have disastrous consequences. The older among them recalled how they had sometimes held commerce with different tribes. On some occasions they had not even spoken the same language but they had managed to get along. Friendly people could make trades without talking at all. Perhaps the Noi settlers could be dealt with as well. They did not seem hostile. Unfortunately, two of the Noi men already had been killed by "that wild fellow" (meaning Dael). They probably would want vengeance. Yes, blood had been spilt and war must surely be the result. That was the conclusion taking form in the discussion.

Here Zan interjected: "Maybe they can be pacified with apologies or gifts or both." Everybody turned toward him. "The wasp people were like that. They cared more for booty than for vengeance."

"Pacified?" Dael cried in fury. "Let us pacify them forever with our spears and those rock-throwing slings you like so much. Pacified? Do you want to wake up in the night to see our dwellings burning, and while you scramble to find rich gifts to 'pacify' them they carry off your women and children or kill them outright. Our enemies lie in our sight across the lake. They must be destroyed!" Several of Dael's followers applauded this speech, clacking their weapons together and urging each other to battle. But most of the men were silent and refused to be roused.

Old Kragg spoke. His joints were stiff with age and he stood with some difficulty. "Wars once started are not easily ended," he said. "And even if we gain the victory we will have paid for it with our blood. Some who sit here now will sit with us no more. And we might lose! They have their sentinels just as we have ours, and it will be difficult to surprise them."

"They probably sit in council at this moment as we do, planning their attack while we talk of peace like women," Dael growled.

Chul the giant rose: "Let us try to talk with these strangers before we start an unnecessary war. I will go to meet them and see what I can learn. It may be that they do not know who attacked them. It was night when Dael found their camp."

"No, Uncle," Zan said. "Your great form will frighten them and seem like an attack. No, I will go. I speak their language, you don't."

"I speak their language better than you do, Zan," Dael declared. "I lived with them and was at their mercy for two long years!" His face visibly twitched at the memory. "I will go with you."

Dael's offer was not well-received. Everybody knew that Dael's purpose was hardly to seek peace. His presence would only make matters worse. It was decided that Zan-Gah would be the emissary of the Ba-Coro. Zan prepared to depart.

Returning to his hut for some necessities, he suddenly noticed two alarming things: one was the braid of Lissa-Na's red hair lying in plain sight on his bed. The other was that Pax was nowhere to be seen. He immediately understood what had happened. Asking several women if they knew where his wife went, two of them told him that she went north with her spear. North was Zan's direction. Pax was heading where he was now going—toward the Noi camp. She was in real danger, and he was busy with his diplomatic mission. He would have to deal with both concerns at once.

As Zan departed for the Noi settlement he tried to guess exactly which way Pax would have gone. It seemed likely that she would stay close to the lake. Trees hung over its lovely surface, but there was a narrow beach where it was easy to walk. Zan resolved to travel in the general direction of the Noi, while keeping an eye out for his wife as he went. Yet he knew very well that he would not find her unless she wanted to be found. Her amazing skill in stalking consisted of her ability to remain unperceived even to the keen senses of ever-watchful animals. She could be anywhere in the woods, observing him at that very moment. Zan looked around at the many-colored broadleaf trees that made this country such a paradise. Every species had its own color, so that each stood out against the others in a splendid array. If Pax were there she was not yet ready to be found; but Zan allowed that she might show herself in time. He wanted to call out her name over and over again, but it was too dangerous. Still he whispered it fairly loudly on several occasions, hoping for a response. There was none.

Had Zan hurried on his errand he might have gotten to the Noi dwellings before darkness fell, but he was lingering along the way in hope of finding Pax. Thus it was that he had to enter their camp at night, guided in the dark by their campfires. Their guards spotted him and took him prisoner before he could say a word or tell his purpose in being there. At night he seemed like an enemy and a spy, and to make matters worse he was soon recognized as the "demon boy" who had a double. His captors were thinking he was Dael whom they had so long held captive.

For all their fierce courage, the Noi were terrified of twins and still remembered the day they had seen Zan and Dael side by side for the first time. It had looked to them like a magical double vision. Their fear had enabled Zan, his brother, and Lissa-Na to escape when their capture or slaughter appeared certain. At that time it seemed to the Noi warriors pursuing them that the youth who had long been their captive had the power to reproduce himself, perhaps into an army of spearmen. They did not now realize that this was his twin and not Dael, nor did it matter to them.

Zan, who spoke their language imperfectly, tried to tell them that he had come as a messenger with peaceful intent, but their fear, the lateness of the hour, and the fact that everybody seemed to be speaking and shouting at the same time, completely overwhelmed any attempt to communicate. A chieftain gave direction and Zan was seized and bound to a tree face-first. Both his arms and legs were wrapped around the tree trunk and tied together, so that his feet were not allowed to touch the ground. Zan was left for the night in great discomfort, which soon grew into real pain.

While he was in this helpless tied-up position, some of the Noi men began to torment him with sharp spears, and one fierce-faced warrior took delight in touching him with a burning stick, his cruel face glowing as he approached. Not so long ago they had tortured Dael, and now they were torturing Zan for their amusement. Zan tried to talk yet again to tell them his errand, but none would listen. At last the old chief who had had Zan bound drove the tormentors away, and after a time the camp was slumbering except for two guards and Zan himself, who was too miserable to sleep.

The fires were slowly going out and all was quiet until, at a very late hour, a vague crashing sound was heard in the bushes nearby. At once the two guards, who were on the verge of snoring, were alert, grabbing torches and spears and heading in the direction of the noise. Then there was another crunching sound somewhat farther off in the brush, and the men were in its depths, visible from a distance in the enveloping darkness by their flaring torches. That was when Zan, unable to support himself, was startled by a soft but urgent whisper close to his ear: "Come, Zan!"

"I can't come anywhere," Zan groaned, half deprived of breath. He was aware of delicate fingers untying him and he knew to whom they and the soft voice belonged. With perhaps more joy than he had ever uttered it, he pronounced his wife's name, "Pax!" and fell to the ground. For the moment he was too weak to support himself.

A handful of pebbles cast in the brush had been enough to divert the attention of the guards. Pax, like a spirit, had slipped into the middle of the camp, released her bound and exhausted husband, and sustained him as they retreated into the woods. They were far away before Zan was even missed, and the guards did not know how he had gotten away. They suspected that his "double" had invisibly come to release him, fearfully conjecturing what a powerful magician he must be. Which way had they gone? They guessed the easiest path, but were too frightened to pursue. Pax had been clever enough not to take the obvious route anyway. Instead, by the light of the moon, she brought Zan to a hidden grove of dappled trees where, as dawn broke, they stopped to rest.

"I am so glad to see you, Pax, but why did you leave?" He knew very well why. She did not have to say that she did not wish to live with a man who loved somebody else, but she did. Zan admitted that he had once loved Lissa-Na. "But that was before I had even met you."

"Then why did you so reverently keep a lock of her hair? Because you adore her memory! You wish I had gorgeous red hair so you could love me."

Zan was not a demonstrative person. He truly loved his wife, but he felt awkward speaking about it. Besides, he had spent an agonizing, sleepless night, and felt half dead. He hurt all over. He desperately needed to sleep, and the green turf of that secluded spot was so inviting that he almost collapsed onto it. Far too exhausted to talk, he immediately dozed off next to where Pax sat. When he awoke it was full day, and Pax was gone.

Zan looked around with sleepy eyes. He was absolutely alone in the middle of the thicket. It was an exceptionally lovely place owing to the trees' unusual character. Their bark was silvery as was the underside of the leaves while the top surface of each leaf was a dark green, almost black. The stem of every leaf was flat rather than round, which caused them to tremble, so that every time the wind changed the leaves turned from dark green to silver and back again. With one gust the whole forest would change color, and with another change back again. Zan rose and peered into the sparkling copse, trying in vain to see which way his wife had gone. The breezes moved this way and that and the leaves showed their under-side. Dark green, silver. Dark, silver.

Ignoring the danger of being heard by his foes, he called her name loudly with some desperation in his voice: "Pax! Pax!" and as he searched through the ever-changing trees, he realized how much he loved her and how empty and bereft his life would be if she didn't come back. Then he saw a white feather on the ground, which was surely the one she had found on the bridge when she had been so frightened of the height. He remembered how she had put away her fear and picked the feather up, and how she had tucked it in her garment while the wind blew wildly over the abyss.

Pax was there somewhere in the thicket. Looking into the dense wood, Zan could not see very far, but maybe he could hear her movements. He listened. He heard nothing. He called again and yet again. Only dark, silver. Dark, silver. Dark, silver. Many minutes went by. Zan was in despair, certain that she would not come back to him. He could see no point in staying any longer, and turned toward the south where his people were.

As he started to walk sadly home, the wind began blowing again and then suddenly, silently, she was there, standing like a statue directly in front of him among the vertical trunks. Where had she come from? She was looking straight at him, her gentle face absolutely placid though her cheeks were wet. Dark, silver. Dark, silver.

Her appearance seemed magical. Only four paces separated them and Zan ran to embrace his wife. "Oh Pax," he cried with more passion than was usual to him. "Never leave me. I love you more than my poor words can say. You know I am not a talker." He held her close and she did not resist. Dark, silver.

"I am not a talker either, Zan," she said, running her fragile fingers through his hair as his mother had once done. "I could not tell you how painfully I felt your attraction to Lissa—not only lately but for a long while. I wondered how you could possibly love me. I am such a skinny, brown little thing—like a small nut that is not worth opening. And Lissa was so beautiful. How could you even notice me beside her loveliness?" Dark, silver.

"Oh, no, Pax," he said, his arm around her now so he could speak softly in her ear. "You *are* beautiful—as lovely as she—but different, slender, and more delicate. Were she living I would not prefer her. I will throw the braid of hair into the fire!"

For a moment Pax said nothing, thinking about his words, and even wondering if she should go away after all. Wouldn't Lissa's memory always stand between them? Could she really believe Zan's reassurances? She did not know whether they were sincere or merely uttered in the heat of the moment. But Pax had one great advantage over Lissa-Na; she was alive and poor Lissa was dead. At last Pax replied, softly touching his hand: "Don't destroy it, Zan. It is all we have left of Lissa and she was a friend. Keep it. We should look at it once in a while...but not too often." Dark, silver.

"I feared that I had lost you forever. I well knew that you would not live with a man who loved another. And suddenly there you were! Why did you return, Pax, if you thought...?"

"Where could I go, Zan? Besides, I had to come back."

"Why?"

"Because...because I am carrying your child."

Dark, silver. Dark, silver. Dark, silver.

15 THE TUSKS

Morda was a large and powerful man, respected if not feared by his people. His grand figure was made larger by the bulky and hairy animal skin he wore winter and summer. It was the pelt of a young musk ox that had been run from its herd and felled by wolves. Morda and his numerous relations had disposed of the grey predators with fire and taken the still-warm conquest for themselves. Morda kept the pelt and loved it. Its dark color was hardly distinguishable from his own long hair and beard, so that it almost seemed an extension of his shaggy mane. The man's habitually frowning eyebrows were shaggy too.

Morda's hut was set up on a rise overlooking the others of his tribe. It was the largest of any dwelling of the Ba-Coro, commanding a fine view of the lake. The house was built from seven saplings lashed together at the top, with walls and roof made of interwoven branches smeared over with mud. One side was mostly open to view the shelters of his fellows, and just as Morda was a large and dominating elder, so did his sizable abode seem to rule over the other huts.

He was a man who liked authority. Morda would bear no insolence from his large family or anyone else. Toward the other elders he could be icy, arrogant, or fierce according to his mood. He was always on a competitive footing with them, frequently enough imagining himself slighted or insulted by people who probably would not have dared to offend.

Morda's proudest possession was the pair of mammoth tusks he had laboriously taken from the slaughtered animal the winter before. He and his wife had dragged them many miles; and he had twice risked his life to carry them on his shoulders across the great gulch when the freezing wind and stupefying height would have deterred a less powerful and determined man.

What were they good for? They were too large to be wielded as weapons, and too hard to be easily cut into any useful item. And they were heavy! But Morda valued them greatly for a less practical reason: they were objects of prestige. Their value was in display, bringing honor to him that displayed them.

Morda dug a small round pit on each side of his doorway, the simple opening of his hut, and planted one tusk in each hole. How splendid they looked! The great pointed forms made a white decorative arch on either side that seemed to say: "Dignity and authority live here!" But after a day or two they fell over, either bumped by children or merely of their own weight. There was no dignity in that! Morda put them up again, and again they fell over. Then he propped them with forked branches and they stayed in position as long as no one came too near.

The tusks were in place when two strangers walked into the presence of the Ba-Coro dwellings one sunshine morning. The sentinels were asleep and the visitors sauntered right past them into the center of the camp. They were tall, goodly men with great bushes of hair, each carrying a spear much longer than his height—elegant as well as dangerous weapons. Rydl was awake at the time, working studiously on a new kind of animal trap, and the newcomers greeted him. Rydl looked up and there they stood looming over him, spears in hand. Rydl was surprised at their sudden appearance, as well as the language they used, which he recognized as the tongue of the Noi. Only he and the twins spoke it, so maybe it was lucky that he of all people had been addressed.

The strangers wanted to talk to the leaders of the Ba-Coro, and a meeting was arranged before anyone had eaten. They were soon surrounded by babbling men, women, and children, all very much excited by the novelty of foreign visitors, and impressed by their long spears. Soon the Noi men and a group of prominent members of the Ba-Coro were sitting in or around the door of Morda's dwelling, with many others gathered nearby out of eager curiosity. Their spears were left leaning against the hovel.

Rydl served as interpreter. He was not used to being the center of attention, but now all eyes were on him as well as the visitors. The taller of the new guests declared their reasons for coming. "We, the Noi people, are prepared for war, but we do not wish it. Why do you attack us?" When Rydl translated these words the men present looked at each other, unsure of what the speaker was talking about.

"We have not attacked you or you would not be here," Morda responded with a sneer, and there were grunts of assent. "We are a warlike people. We fought the wasp people and won. Where are they now?" While Rydl translated, Morda was looking this way and that as if the vanquished wasp men might actually be in the hut. "As for you, we do not fear you. We wish for peace and sent you our man to tell you so, but you tied and afflicted him instead of listening to his message."

"He was a demon. Only fire will destroy him," said the taller of the two men, dismissively. "But one of your warriors fell on ours and killed two. It was a cowardly act to slay sleeping men. If you give the killer to us, we will make peace with you. If not, prepare for war!"

Rydl translated, and a stir of voices followed the threatening words. Zan-Gah, now recovered from his ordeal as captive, stepped forward and he was angry. The two messengers recognized him and stood back in real fear. If they had had their weapons at hand, they might have used them to defend themselves. "We have never been your enemies, but you yourselves have been," Zan said in their language, wrath in his eyes. "You held my brother prisoner for two years, and now his mind is filled with vengeance. From my single night in your hands I can begin to imagine how you treated him. Yes, he killed men who had tormented him, and it will be difficult to hold him back from further harm. But it is your own fault!"

"Give us that man and we will be content."

"No!"

It was fortunate that Dael was not present. He had left with a few of his friends the day before to revisit the volcano. Otherwise, he would have assaulted the two Noi men on the spot. The messengers turned to go. Several of the people stepped aside to let them pass.

"Wait," said Zan-Gah, subduing his anger. The pair turned again. "There is some justice in your position. But there is justice in ours too. Let us come to an agreement. Is there anything that we can give you that will satisfy you and calm your desire for revenge? The man you seek is not entirely guilty, so let us settle on something that will please and satisfy your people. Then we can make peace. But we will fight before we give him up, and beware our weapons. The wasp people thought themselves stronger than we, and you see their fate!"

The Noi messengers were still afraid of Zan's supposed magical powers, and, too, they had always considered the wasp people more powerful and warlike than themselves. Now they were negotiating with the people who had overcome this fierce race and who apparently could bring magic into any battle. They asked for a moment to consider Zan-Gah's proposal and stepped outside the hut.

No doubt the two messengers felt a certain shame in backing off from their demands; and considered that they would have to come home with something extraordinary if they and their people were not to look like fools. Just then a child in the crowd sat on one of Morda's tusks and it dropped to the ground. Morda heard it collapse and came running out of his hut, looking at it with dismay and disgust. Meanwhile, the Noi men were gazing at the two objects with wonder. They had never seen a mammoth, and although they recognized that these were some kind of teeth, did not know what they were. They only could see that the creature they came from must have been larger than anything they had ever beheld. They looked at them and felt their smooth surface, deeply impressed. Then they both said almost at the same time: "Give us these and we will be satisfied."

Morda stiffened and frowned. Two glowering tigers became visible in the dark caverns beneath his shaggy eyebrows. Even before their alien words were interpreted Morda knew what these men wanted; and he had no intention of giving up his prized possessions. The gigantic tusks looked so handsome in front of his house, and told the world the kind of man he was! And how he had labored to chop them from the stinking corpse of the mammoth! "Choose another gift," he snorted. "These stay here. I carried them on my own back at the risk of my life, and I certainly will not give them up to strangers!"

Risking Morda's anger—and he was already angry— Zan spoke up: "These twin tusks have a magical power. As long as you have the two of them together, no demon can trouble you with his double." Morda saw then and there that he was going to lose both tusks. He had hoped to content them with only one. The Noi men were fascinated. They conferred in a whisper. Then turning to the others they said they would be satisfied if the gift were accompanied by a general apology. Rydl told them what they were saying.

"We are sorry," several men said in feigned contrition, nodding their heads and glancing at each other. Their gestures conveyed apology. The messengers were content.

Perhaps if the tusks had not been so easily knocked down Morda would have resisted parting with his treasures. If truth be told, he was sick of worrying about them. Nevertheless, he demanded to be compensated by the rest of the Ba-Coro if he were to give them up. Chul understood Morda's self-importance and congratulated him on his "noble sacrifice."

"You are saving our people from a dreadful war, and we thank you. It was bravely done!" he said, putting his ponderous hand on Morda's shoulder. Several others said similar pleasing things.

Morda grunted. He was highly flattered by this praise, but had determined to be discontented until he received some other reward besides congratulations. Meanwhile the Noi men were loading the tusks on their shoulders. The great weight of the objects made them all the more valuable to them. They awkwardly grabbed their spears and left the way they had come, singing a rhythmic song as laboring men often do, greatly pleased.

Zan also praised Morda for his sacrifice, and promised him the lion skin—his own most prized possession—to compensate him for what he had given up. It was the magnificent pelt of the lioness he had killed when he was a boy. Zan had accomplished that feat almost by accident, and everybody still honored him for it and called him Zan-Gah. The hide was not that difficult to part with. Zan privately rejoiced to have saved his brother, realizing that events might well have taken a different turn. He also rejoiced that Dael had not been present.

16 DAEL'S POWER

When Dael returned from the fire-mountain, half his men walked on one side of him and half on the other. This formation reflected a new fact: Dael was indisputably their leader. And he was more. He was their prophet and their seer. It appeared that they would follow him blindly, so much were they in awe of his magnetic and forceful personality. His authority, which had been considerable before the last visit to the volcano, was cemented by a new stunning episode experienced in the mountain's shadow. Dael had fainted. Dael had seemed dead. And then he arose with a look of the other world on his face. None of the men had ever encountered anyone who could communicate with spirits in the land of the dead. It was frightening, sinister, and yet empowering to know one who had made the voyage to that dark region and returned to tell what he had learned.

This time Dael was not docile. Perhaps he would have been if Zan had been there to guide his waking thoughts. But now the exhilarating experience of being admired to the point of adoration, combining with the harrowing intensity of his passions, lent him a new dynamic confidence. Upon awakening he almost glowed with an unearthly feeling, so that he hardly knew where he was. He believed that he had indeed communicated with spirits, and was entitled to the authority his men gave him. With an enlarged sense of self he intoned commands, and they were obeyed with alacrity.

Dael's followers were mostly young men—apt and vigorous hunters and warriors. Almost all of them had some time ago scarified their faces in swirling patterns in imitation of their master. Together they composed a formidable and frightening cadre. They reentered the Ba-Coro camp as if they were its rulers, and everybody looked up. Had they been an invading force they could hardly have garnered more notice. They intended no mischief toward their own, but Dael had deliberately made a show of force before their assembled eyes. He sent his men to their huts knowing that they would come when he called them.

Dael was about to return to his own crude dwelling place when he chanced to espy Morda wearing his newly acquired lion skin. Asking him how he happened to have "Zan-*Gaaahh's* property," Morda explained; and as he did Dael visibly changed, almost exploding with anger. He was enraged that peace had been made with his mortal enemies during his absence; but that the Ba-Coro had *apologized,* as Morda sheepishly confessed, infuriated him to the point of danger. Dael declared he would have consented to be torn to pieces before making such concessions. Then he learned that the proposal had come first from Zan-Gah, and he was genuinely mortified, and full of wrath. But suddenly Dael said no more on the subject, although a furious turmoil boiled within. "No brother of mine!" he was thinking to himself. He was determined that the peace settlement would not stand, and as evening approached he quietly called his followers together.

Their huts were somewhat to the north of the general encampment, and being apart they could confer without it being immediately apparent to the others of the Ba-Coro. Dael spoke to his men with glittering eyes and impassioned brow, denouncing the peacemakers and sending the thoughts of his men in a new aggressive direction. By nightfall the schism of the Ba-Coro, which had been trying to heal itself, was wider than ever. Dael didn't care.

"We will not abide by this shameful agreement," he concluded with iron determination. "Bring your spears and by morning we will be in position to attack our enemies. Then come what may! The other warriors (cowards!) will join us in the fight or perish at the hands of the Noi. They will fight, I promise you! We have superior weapons and we need not fear them."

Dael knew his men had long since practiced to proficiency with their spear-throwers. He had made the significant discovery that superior weapons sometimes were as important as superior courage—and his faction had both. In fact Dael had long anticipated war with the Noi, and now he would initiate it with a provocative surprise attack.

Dael had another power and it came decisively into play. Dael could talk to the spirits, and vowed to enlist their aid. His fainting fits were becoming more common, brought on by hysterical extremes of emotion and his intense personal conviction that he could contact the lower world whenever he wished. As he readied his men, he suddenly fell to the ground, writhed, foamed at the mouth, and seemed dead. When he rose to inspire his followers, he described visions of the spirit world, uttering wild mystic messages of courage and attack. Soon the men were in frenzy, and were almost prepared to fight with their own kinsmen. But Dael urged them north towards the camp of the Noi.

A full moon illuminated the forest, but it was still too dark to travel easily. A group of twenty men would necessarily make noise tramping through the woods, and Dael's efforts to quiet them were less than successful. Moreover they were pulsing out rhythmic grunts to fire their courage, as men of war will. They had worked themselves into a state of exaltation, perhaps necessary for battle but not conducive to an effective surprise maneuver.

At length, having marched most of the way, Dael stopped his band and commanded that they quietly rest until dawn approached, with the thought that they could resume the assault once it was light enough to see. No one built a fire, and the half-exhausted men fell asleep. Dael woke them with the first light.

Dael was a man of abrupt action, not at all inclined to make careful plans. He and his men, under the spur of rage and sudden impulse, had marched off to ambush the Noi without considering the problems that night presented. They might well have been ambushed themselves! Their progress had been heard and observed, and when they arrived at the Noi village, warriors stood in their path ready to defend it. A wall of spearmen held their lengthy weapons erect and ready.

A tremor passed through Dael's entire band. The defenders were several times more numerous than they! Dael himself was not subject to fear. From where he stood he could see Morda's tusks already mounted in a place of honor, and the sight infuriated him. Calling his men to second him, he flung his spear and his followers did the same. The spear-throwing device Rydl had invented gave them an advantage, for it enabled their weapons to fly farther and faster than those of the Noi. But the distance separating the two hosts was not great enough to give them much benefit, and the Noi, sustaining this assault and retaining their weapons, charged at the invaders.

There were too many to resist. Dael's men broke and ran lest they be surrounded and slaughtered. Dael, slower to depart than the others, was separated from them and fled in a different direction into the woods, followed by his pet wolves, which had trailed the entire way. The surprise attack had been a failure. Three of his own had been left behind dead, and three Noi warriors were grievously wounded. Now alone, he was pursued by six Noi men, and there was nothing to do but run and hide if he could.

Dael went crashing through the forest with ample strides, the Noi men hotly after him. His wolves, large, dangerous looking animals, ran behind and possibly seemed to the men to be chasing him too. These desert people were unfamiliar with the wolf and afraid of it, but that did not slow them down and they ran with all their might. Dael came to a creek and ran nimbly over the fallen log that spanned it. His pets waded after him through the shallow water, determined to keep him company. One warrior threw his spear, which might well have pierced its target had not a low branch deflected it. But the chase would soon be over. Dael's flight was arrested by a high, overhanging embankment and he was forced to run along side of it, looking for an escape. In another minute he would be surrounded and killed.

Yet at the base of the rising wall of earth and mossy rock was a hollow—a hole half stuffed with leaves. Maybe it was a cave! Dael fairly dove into it, his wolves worming their way after him on their bellies. Unluckily it took but a moment or two for his enemies to find the opening and note the marks of entry. Meanwhile Dael tried to see the extent of the hollow by the dim light coming solely from the opening. He immediately determined that it was not a cavern, only an animal's den, as the foul smell of decaying flesh and some animal bones told him. Dael's pursuers had him trapped, and had only to follow him through the hole if they dared. Dael got ready to fight. Seizing a large thighbone, he prepared to brain the first entrant.

The Noi warriors were gathered outside, poking their long spears into the opening, when Dael had an idea. Crouching down in a corner of the den, and holding his pets on either side of him in his strong arms, he began howling and goading them as he had often done in sport.

The animals responded with shrill yelps and wails that reverberated within the hollow: *Arroo-roo-roo. Yi-yi. Arroo-roo.* The uncanny resonance emerging from the earth was hardly to be described!

Fierce and brave as the Noi warriors were, they were also superstitious. Things unfamiliar puzzled and disconcerted them. What were they to make of the strange tattooed man who kept company with wolves? Had he changed himself into a beast too? What was the nature of the magic these alien people wielded, and how could it be resisted? "Let us bring fire here to burn the wolf man out," said one.

And so they did, but by the time they brought it Dael and his howling pets were gone.

17 RYDL'S GARDEN

Not far from the camp of the Ba-Coro there was a moist field with a gentle rise in the middle. Capping this dryer knoll lay a single patch of an unusually intense green that, even from a distance, stood out like a precious jewel. A sea of muted browns, ochres, and grays surrounded and set off this island of gleaming color, which was not very large—about the length of three spears. Every day Rydl could be seen on or near it, as if it were his private treasure.

The bright spot was grain that Rydl had planted and nurtured. He had painstakingly uprooted every wild plant from a small area, pulling out each weed and grass while working and loosening the soil to receive the seeds he had saved. He understood instinctively that the weeds had to be kept from coming back. Rydl was introducing a new population of plants, and the alien competition had to be expelled. Laboring to see if he could produce grain on purpose rather than finding it by accident, his efforts were rewarded with a ripening crop. Rydl could visualize a time when the entire meadow would be this same green color, and his adopted people could eat without searching—eat what they wanted and store the rest.

But the war Dael and his men had so recklessly begun threatened to bring an end to Rydl's efforts. He would himself have to prepare for a fight, and it seemed likely that the field chosen for a battle would be the very one he had selected for his experiment.

It turned out to be so. This space lay on the path connecting the two opposing settlements, and since the flinging of spears requires arm room, both the Ba-Coro and the Noi tended to think of it as the place where a battle could be fought. And if everybody anticipated it, how could it fail to come to pass? Both peoples were preparing, training, making weapons, and practicing with them. Every night either tribe might hear the drums and chants of the other from across the lake, and each night the sounds were more belligerent and intense. Sometimes the separate rhythms mixed together in painful cacophony, already at war with each other.

Neither side challenged or informed the other, and yet, as if by agreement, both sides appeared on edges of the field on the same morning, standing in wait of the other's attack. The drums had told them what to expect—not in any explicit way, but when by night violent percussion is engendering a wild dance of war, who fails to foresee the approaching combat?

Dael's men, scarified, shaven, and in an aggressive posture, appeared first on their side of the field, not long after joined by all the warriors of the Ba-Coro. The latter had the advantage of superior weapons, being well armed with spears, spear throwers, and slings. But the group as a whole was weighed down by the consciousness that it was they (or rather Dael's faction) who had broken an honorable truce. The Noi men appeared opposite, emerging quietly and rather suddenly from a wall of trees. Their abrupt appearance as if from nowhere made a frightening impression, for they were very numerous. Moreover they were tall, strong men, moving in concert in a single formation which indicated decisiveness and unity. Theirs was the attitude of aggrieved victims of a naked betrayal. They surely had right on their side!

Chul, whose huge bulk alone was like a weapon, led an attack. He did not wait for the Noi men to come into range with their spears, but ordered a fusillade of stones to be fired with slings before the enemy spears could present any danger. If the Noi meant to attack, they would have to do it under the storm of rocks flung with a speed and power they had never seen. Despite the repeated volleys of stones, they did attack on the run so that they could use their weapons before too many had been struck down. A number already were felled, but the Noi were brave and fierce combatants, not likely to take blows without delivering some in return.

The Noi men fought fully as well as the Ba-Coro, but they had a single fatal weakness: they were frightened, even paralyzed, by the unfamiliar. Once, just after Dael had been released from captivity, he and Zan had been able to face down ten strong Noi warriors because they were terrified of twins. The men had fled as if confronted by twin demons!

Now weapons were being used against them that they had never seen before. The Ba-Coro slings had stunned them with an unexpected barrage; and the launching of deadly spears from a hand-held throwing implement not only devastated their numbers with dead and wounded, but deeply demoralized them with the sense that some unfamiliar power or magic was being exploited.

Chul's gigantic size and bellowing voice also seemed strange and magical. Had Zan and Dael still looked at all alike, that alone might have turned the battle. Zan was well aware of the difference that might have made, but Dael, who had deliberately and dramatically altered his appearance, seemed unconcerned with the advantage they had lost.

Despite their superstitious dread, the men of Noi had come to fight. Spears were being hurled on both sides, but the Ba-Coro were gaining ground. After much brutal battle and slaughter on the field—in which Rydl's garden was thoroughly trampled—the Noi began to withdraw into the trees. Dael and his men were particularly forward in pursuing them, but once in the woods the benefit of their superior weapons was lost and the Noi were in a position to strike with sudden ambushes, so that soon the Ba-Coro withdrew too. Although they had driven the Noi away for the present, the battle had been indecisive; and the casualties were such that both sides knew that they could not sustain too many like it.

Poor Rydl, who was too gentle to be a good warrior, had received a spear in the thigh, as Chul once had in battle. But Rydl was no Chul. The delicate young man collapsed onto the ground groaning in pain while blood gushed from his wound. Zan-Gah, seeing him fall, sped to his aid. He would carry him to safety, but it was absolutely necessary first to extract the spear from the wound. This Zan did as quickly as he could, ignoring Rydl's scream of agony. He lifted the frail body of his fainting friend on his shoulders and carried him off, leaving behind a puddle of Rydl's blood—which stained crimson the green swath that Rydl had so lovingly planted.

Seeking a safe spot, at length Zan leaned Rydl against an immense fallen trunk whose jagged, exposed roots sprang upwards over their heads. It offered some temporary shelter.

When Zan returned to the fight, it was already ending. Weary men, some themselves wounded, were helping to carry back the dead. Among the numerous fatal casualties were Morda and two of his sons. The young brothers were still handsome in death, and Morda still fierce and darkly frowning. Chul was hurt too. A Noi warrior had charged the giant with his long spear, but Chul had dodged the main thrust, slaughtering his assailant as he passed. Now, two men were bringing Morda's once powerful body to a place of burial while Chul, although wounded, carried the two slain boys, one on each shoulder.

Rydl also was carried back, half dead. Unlike Morda and the others, he had no family to grieve over him or to leap to his aid. But one who loved him, forgetting all of her coldness and reserve, screamed aloud when she saw his limp body borne from the field. Running to him in great distress, she threw herself on him with sobs.

It was Sparrow. The sight of her bleeding friend overwhelmed her. Now she abruptly rediscovered the depth of her feelings for the wounded man, and she could not hide it. But things had changed; she was needed now! For several days she silently tended Rydl's wounds, fed him by sips during his fever, sustained him in his weakness, and lay night and day by his side. With her loving help, Rydl would survive his hurt and the dangerous infection that followed. But he would be crippled for the rest of his life, limping deeply and supporting himself on a staff. He was lucky to be alive.

Long before Rydl could stand, when beads of sweat still glistened on his brow in token of his pain and delirium, when he was still struggling to form his words, he apologized to Sparrow, breathing heavily: "I am sorry, gentle bird, that I could not love you as you did me, and that I am entirely undeserving of your affection, unworthy of your tenderness." He needed a moment to recover his breath. At the time he was in agony and did not expect to live. "You must see by now that I could never love or marry any woman, not even one as lovely and mild as you. I have cared for you as a friend, truly I have, but it was not in my nature to do more."

Sparrow did not try to reply. She only pressed close to him as if she were indeed his wife, passed her slender arm over his heaving, upturned chest, and wept.

18 SIRAKA-FINAKA

Siraka-Finaka, Chul's short wife, had grown very fat but she was inwardly unchanged. Chul towered over her, but only in physical stature. It might be said that her forceful personality towered over her husband's quieter one, and that her sharp tongue overpowered his slow one. The mother of three girls, she cared for little else, and was always fearful that they might lose their father if she did not curb her husband's warlike ways. She did not hesitate to let Chul know that she considered the new war to be foolish and unnecessary; and her wrath against Dael and his followers knew no bounds.

"You are an elder of our people," said she. "Why do you permit a renegade band to make policy for us on matters of this importance? Your nephew—I mean Dael, not the good one—will get you killed. Then what would become of your family? Morda lost his great tusks and then he lost his two sons, and then he lost his life! Zan-Gah could die in battle too, and then what would Pax and her baby do? She is with child, you know."

"With child?"

"With child, you blind oaf! We should have turned Dael over to the Noi when they asked us to, instead of defending him and humbling ourselves. You must realize that he is crazed, and I think you are too! My dear friend, Lissa-Na, who died trying to give a son to that brute, was of these same people we are trying to destroy. We did not hate her. Why do we hate them? If she had lived she would have found a way to settle this mess, which you are only making worse. Why can't we come to terms with them instead of fighting? Would you like me to wash your wound again? Turn around, you old fool."

While she bathed the gash on his side, Chul thought over her words. He could find little to disagree with, but at the same time the idea of giving his brother's son to the enemy—an enemy who had kept and tortured him when he was a mere child, and certainly would slay him once he was in their hands—was not only unjust, it was unthinkable. Still, he resolved that Dael had to be controlled. He could not be allowed to foment further mischief between the two peoples. When Dael started trouble, the rest of them inherited the consequences!

He remembered Lissa-Na's fine qualities and wondered if others of her people had goodness too. Was it not so with the Ba-Coro? Among his own people there were some who were wise and deliberate, others who were stupid and rash. There were cruel people among them as well as kind. Even the twins—even Zan-Gah and Dael—sprung from the same womb on the same day, showed that people who ought to be alike actually could be very different. Must it not be so with the Noi as well?

But even if it was so, even if the Noi divided into good and bad, it was uncertain which group had the upper hand among them. For that matter, who had the upper hand among the Ba-Coro? People not only disagreed with each other, they often were at odds with themselves, leaning one way by day and another by night. Now that Dael spoke to spirits he could tell his men what they wanted. Surely there were good and bad spirits too.

Dael had tried a surprise attack with disastrous results. "Crazy as he is, he is not likely to try that again," Chul said aloud to himself. The Noi were alerted and could not be surprised easily, and Dael's following was smaller than it had been before. They would not be difficult to restrain. In the latest conflict both sides had suffered severe casualties, and neither seemed anxious to mount an attack. Perhaps it was a good time to talk.

Chul wanted to act alone. He intended to walk into the Noi camp all by himself and speak to them man-to-man. But he reflected that the other elders would be angry if he did not confer with them first, so he approached them one at a time. They quietly agreed that someone should go to the Noi with an overture of peace, but Chul would need a translator, and there was no one but Zan-Gah.

Zan was consulted and he groaned at the thought of returning to the Noi. He had no desire to become their captive and victim again, having barely survived his recent visit. And he questioned the wisdom of Chul's resolution to go. At length he was prevailed upon to take the risk, not wanting his uncle to go alone. It was too dangerous. He kissed Pax warmly and tried to calm her fears. Her pregnancy was beginning to show.

The plan was kept secret from Siraka-Finaka. Chul knew very well that she would object to the father of the family taking on such dangers. By accident she heard about the mission, however, and refused to permit it. Chul would stay at home and let someone else go with Zan-Gah! Small as she was she had great authority with her husband, and this time she was determined to use it.

The marital quarrel that ensued was almost violent, but it did not last long. Siraka-Finaka finally declared that if her husband were fool enough to go, she would go along too! She was not joking. All of Chul's protestations and growling threats could not change her mind. At last Chul agreed, providing that she came secretly and kept her tongue from wagging. He knew he would be the butt of every man's guffaw if they discovered that he had been accompanied by his woman. Chul was more concerned about disgrace than the very real possibility that none of them would return alive. But they went. Their children were left in the care of Zan-Gah's parents and the three quietly departed, Siraka-Finaka struggling bravely to keep up with her plump little legs.

When they approached the camp of the Noi, they were immediately taken captive, but this time the presence of a woman cast their sudden arrival in a different light. It was apparent that these visitors intended no harm, especially in broad daylight. Zan's former visit had been at night and seemed suspicious. Despite Chul's great size he could do no harm, surrounded as he was by Noi warriors. His wife's short figure was an object of mirth, and the very presence of a woman on such a mission seemed ridiculous—but not threatening. Siraka-Finaka's attendance probably saved their lives.

The party of three was conducted to a circle of elders. These were once handsome but now craggy men who resembled nothing so much as the elders of the Ba-Coro. Chul began in his deep bass and Zan-Gah interpreted. Siraka-Finaka knew enough to hold her peace. "Many have died," Chul said, "and many more have been wounded. We did not wish to waste lives in needless battle, but it happened. It was the fault of a small group, which will be punished! They broke the peace, not we."

Chul did not know how Dael's group could be "punished" but he said what he knew he had to say if there were to be any hope of a settlement. "Let there be no more fighting, but let each of us raise our families in peace. We give our promise that we will not attack you if you do not attack us." Chul and Zan knew that their position lacked substance because it was the Ba-Coro who had violated the truce. But what more could they say?

There were murmurs among the Noi. Chul's offer actually was tempting to their diminished ranks. Yet it would not be accepted. Two men came forward and the youngest spoke out. He was a tall and goodly man, one of those who had asked for the tusks of Morda when he had been among the Ba-Coro. His aged father, a respected chieftain, stood behind him: "Why should we believe you?" the younger man said with some contempt in his voice. "Your wretches attacked sleeping men, and later came at us in force to kill and burn. We sent them on their way, and will do the same with the rest of you!" Several of the Noi huffed their assent.

"We had not provoked you, but you made war on us. Still we came to you with an offer of peace and you see what came of it! The latest fight cost us dear, but we have learned valuable lessons and are not afraid. We will not trust you again. You are not decent people. And we will not wait patiently for you to assault us, but beware our attack!" Again, loud grunts of the elders signaled assent and unity. "We burn our dead tomorrow. Come to the field of battle the day after and you will find us there. For now we release you as *honor* demands." He stressed the word sarcastically, and even Siraka-Finaka understood the implication: The Noi had honor; the Ba-Coro had it not.

The older man, crowned with a headdress of bright, arching feathers, was obviously an elder of great prestige. "Make no mistake," he added, coming forward with a clenched fist, his long, bending plumes trembling as he spoke. "You cannot frighten us." He glanced at Zan-Gah. "If you have magic we have magic too. You will not destroy us. We will live!" His intense grimace, which deepened his wrinkles and showed his lower teeth, was that of one who had spent his life surviving bitter trials. "We are an ancient people, used to hardships and war. *We will live!*"

Chul, Siraka-Finaka, and Zan-Gah returned to their camp, and Chul told the bad news: The war would continue. The drums began to sound again, clashing against each other over the peaceful surface of the lake. Every male prepared for the approaching confrontation. Still in Siraka-Finaka's mind there was a glimmer of hope. The Noi considered themselves decent and honorable. Who would have known?

19 FUNERAL PYRES

That night great fires were reflected in the beautiful lake, visible from both sides; and all the next day the two peoples smelled each other's funeral pyres. Cremation was permitted in times of war when burial and the building of barrows would take too long. Ashes would be saved and monuments erected, but later, after the fight. There were several corpses to dispose of, but Morda's had a place of special honor, as did his two dead sons, whose mangled bodies were laid on either side of their father. The sons had been Dael's men and their heads were shaved, their limbs and torsos decorated with scar patterns. The surviving sons as well as Morda's brothers had grim expressions harboring thoughts of revenge in the coming battle, while Morda's daughters and his patient wife were melting in tears as a roaring fire reduced their loved ones to nothing.

Dael's sleep was troubled as usual. Among the phantoms that haunted his dreams, one in particular had lately gained ascendancy—so much so that Dael could almost depend upon its appearance. He avoided sleeping, knowing that the specter would come. It was Hurnoa who visited him—or rather her gray, disheveled head, eyes glazed, dripping with blood, and haloed by an eerie light. Dael would toss and thrash, trying desperately to run but curiously unable to move. The head spoke in gravel tones, as Hurnoa had in life. Dael wished he could forget her hateful language but he clearly understood her words—although the sound of her voice seemed weirdly detached from her moving lips: "Why do you not run, Dael? Leave your people in peace. You are no longer one of them. Go to the fire-mountain and throw yourself in." And in a moment he was there on the summit, flinging himself into the fiery heart. He woke up trembling and sweating, and there was Zan.

"Are you all right, Dael?" Zan asked. "What did you dream that disturbed you so? You are still shaking."

"It is with anger then," Dael replied, coming to himself. "I dreamed I had a spear in each hand and was slaying my enemies two at a time, and you were running away."

"Dael," Zan said, "this hatred is not good for you. Isn't it possible for you to put it aside?"

"Don't you hate anyone, Zan-*Gaahh*? Have you never hated someone with all your heart? Maybe you would if you had lived in a cage as I did for two years. If you had been submitted to indignities too shameful to mention, and been fed unspeakable things when you were fed at all. They are cannibals, you know, Zan. At least I think they are," and he began to gag.

Zan put his arm around his brother, who shook to get it off, but Zan did not let go. "Dael, you must forget all that. You know yourself that some of them were not evil people. Lissa-Na was one of them, and who was ever a better person?"

This time Dael did pull loose, wheeling violently and slapping his brother powerfully in the face with the back of his left hand as he turned. "I told you never to speak of her. If you ever mention her name to me in connection with *those*, I will slay you, I promise you. Then I will not have a twin."

Zan was holding his face. Blood was flowing from his nose. He said nothing for a moment, looking at Dael as one might look at a pet that had just bitten him. "You surely will regret doing that," he said at last. He was convinced that his brother would feel sorry for what he did.

Dael understood his words in another sense: "Do you threaten me, you dog? After the fight tomorrow, I will finish you. I will be looking for you. Now would be a good time for you to run away, coward."

Zan left Dael's presence. It was more than he could deal with, and he was indeed running away.

▼ ▼ ▼

Meanwhile Siraka-Finaka was going from one elder to another. She was convinced that the war need not resume, and said so to those who would listen. She also spoke to their wives, hoping that they might use their influence: "This is a conflict begun by Dael and his men without consulting the elders. Let them fight if they must, but I tell you the Noi can be reasoned with." She talked at length to anyone she could corner, but had no success.

Two weeks of rainy weather prevented the intended battle, but no one supposed that it would not occur. By the time the sky cleared and the land was dry enough to walk on, Rydl had passed his climax of fever and had even risen, propped by a crutch and assisted by the dedicated young Sparrow. Siraka-Finaka, with the aid of other peace-loving women of the tribe, continued to urge delay and negotiation, but another challenge was brought by a Noi messenger and the word went out that the fight would resume the next day.

▼ ▼ ▼

The morning began with thunder rumbling from afar, which early wakened both peoples and urged them on to war. A cloudless blue sky gave no sign of further bad weather, yet the ominous rumbling continued. The Ba-Coro appeared on the field at an early hour, but to their surprise the Noi were already there in formal array, occupying the higher center instead of the edge, and thus minimizing the distance that separated them from their enemies. Their objective was to diminish the space so that the Ba-Coro held less of an advantage, being within striking distance.

Both sides were ready to fight. Like a pair of poisonous snakes whose wavering heads are poised to strike each other with lightning speed, or two mighty stallions which, with hooves upraised, prepare to fight for a mate, the armies reared and clashed. Every man had a battle cry, and no spear or stone was flung without a screeching *"heeaughh!"* Deadly blows were struck on both sides, and within minutes the ground was littered with bodies of the fallen. How many had to die before one side or the other of these stubborn combatants would yield or flee? What prize or victory were they fighting to achieve?

These questions found no answers, for something so unexpected happened in the midst and thick of the fight that it astounded and baffled both sides. The furious battle had hardly commenced when there was an explosion of noise louder than any warrior ever in his lifetime had heard. The astonishing sound reverberated and echoed off the granite cliffs, and rang in every ear. It was ten times louder than thunder, and accompanied by a blast of wind that caused the trees to bend and even break, their dead branches to drop with a crash, and their many-colored autumn leaves to shake down, leaving the limbs half bare. The swelling conflict abruptly ceased as both groups looked to the skies with terrified, questioning faces, unable to comprehend this message from their gods.

The Noi warriors were the first to run, and the Ba-Coro did not even think to pursue them. The Noi were unable to deal with unfamiliar things, even those far less formidable; while their opponents were themselves paralyzed with shock and indecision. Dael recognized the voice of his god—the thunder-fit of the fire-mountain— and more than any other he was frozen, stunned, and overwhelmed. His eyes bulged in their sockets and turned upward, and with a face distorted by a paroxysm of emotion he screamed and fell. Later, when the volcano had quieted down, ceasing for a time to void its fiery discharge, Dael's lifeless body was retrieved along with many others. The eruption, now spreading only flakes of gray ashes, coated the dead, the surrounding country, and the once beautiful lake.

Zan, filled with grief, carried the body of his brother home. There were no wounds on it. Only Dael's face was pale and bloodless, his eyes sunken and dark. Apparently he had died a victim of his own tempestuous and harrowing passions. Everyone knew how deeply disturbed he was, nightly dreaming horrific sights, and burdened with emotions deadly even to the strongest man. Dael's vow to kill his twin brother, his own mother's son, had weighed on his secret soul, and above all, the recurrent vision of Hurnoa's bleeding head accused and overpowered him. In the fight Dael had hardly been in contact with reality, and the simultaneous, palpable presence of his two great obsessions brought him down to the ground. Between them, the Noi and the mountain of fire had torn his spirit in two.

Zan and his parents lamented together. Wumna especially wailed Dael's death. This was the second time that she had lost her son. For almost three years she had thought him dead, only to have him brought back to her alive, but with his soul tortured and flayed. Nothing worse could happen to him now. Dael was dead indeed.

Pax stood by to comfort Wumna, Zan, and the others. Chul was there with wet eyes, and Rydl hobbled out as well, supported by Sparrow under one arm. Even in his grief Zan could not but notice that those whom Dael had most disliked among his people were there to lead the mourning. "My poor brother can be hurt no more," he said as much to himself as anyone else. "I never thought him a bad person, only disfigured by his suffering and unhappiness. Before he was taken prisoner, who ever expected anything but kindness and good humor from him? And look what a bitter dish the spirits served him, what poisoned waters they gave him to drink! Hatred destroys, and hate killed my brother along with many others. Now let us burn him with fire and hope that his spirit finds peace."

Dael's men, broken also by the loss of their leader and prophet, solemnly gathered a pile of dry wood, made available in great quantity by the volcanic explosion. Zan lifted Dael on his shoulder, and with the help of Oin and Orah laid him gently atop the funeral pyre. With a prayer to the sky spirit and a hymn for the dead, Zan himself lit it. It was one of fourteen fires, and there was a general lament.

As the flames began to rise from Dael's crackling heap, Zan broke down, sobbing bitter tears for his twin and falling onto his knees beside his mother Wumna, who was already on hers. The wails of grief were so pronounced that no one heard or noticed someone coughing from the smoke and groaning aloud. Only after a moment or two did Zan look up…and there was Dael, removed from his burning pyre and standing next to it as erect as a statue, silent as a ghost.

Dael lived! Dael had come back again! Everyone stared at him in amazement. He had that strange aura of the other world shining from his still-pale face, and looked exactly like what he was—a corpse that had returned to life.

20 DEPARTURE

In the camp of the Ba-Coro, there was more sadness than joy. Siraka-Finaka rejoiced at Dael's revival for his mother's sake, but she sorrowed too—sorrowed at her failure to have prevented a useless and indecisive battle. Many on both sides had been killed, so that the air smelled of funeral pyres and their burning burden. Many more had been wounded, some never to recover.

Two fights had now taken place, and the number of widows had significantly increased; yet there was no end in sight. The third battle—and the fourth, and fifth—were yet to ensue. Siraka-Finaka's husband, Chul, had nearly lost his life, yet now he was preparing to venture out again before his wound was healed! Something needed to be done to end this madness, she decided, but it was useless to talk to the elders who, ever beating the drums of war, actually seemed eager for more incursions.

Siraka was a dwarfish woman, but she had a strong and assertive character, and was used to getting her way. Three days after the battle she made up her mind to take matters into her own hands. She would visit the Noi and talk things over. It cost nothing to talk. Why not try? These people already knew her, she reasoned, and had no fear of her because she was a woman, not a combatant. Perhaps women could accomplish what the men of the tribe could not—or would not.

Siraka went to Agrud, Morda's bereaved wife, and suggested the project. Agrud had enjoyed little enough happiness with her tyrannical mate, but she was still devastated by his death and that of her sons. Softened by grief, she was easily persuaded to go, and asked her sister to go too. At length a delegation of five women secretly left to visit the Noi.

They did not know what to expect. People at war are not likely to be reasonable, but possibly they too were made more pliable by their grief. Perhaps their losses were great enough to give them pause and persuade them to seize an opportunity for peace. It might be also that contact could be made with the Noi women. If they were at all like Lissa-Na, they could be reasoned with. Surely they cared more about their men and their families than about *victory*. Women of every people share the same griefs and sufferings, Siraka thought to herself. They are not interested in dealing wounds, only in preventing or curing them.

Siraka-Finaka and her friends decided that they would not walk directly into the Noi camp, but quietly watch for an opportunity to speak to the Noi women first. Like the Ba-Coro, the Noi women spent a lot of time separated from the men. An initial contact with them might be feasible. If not, they would directly approach the elders. The fact that they spoke a different language did not greatly worry them. People will understand if they really wish to, they decided; and if they are not so inclined, a common language will not help much.

It was early morning when the five left. Ashes of the volcano were still everywhere, although a gentle autumn wind was beginning to disperse them. Siraka-Finaka and her companions trudged along, leaving a trail of footprints in the dust. By noon they had almost arrived. They wished to be cautious without appearing sneaky or stealthy, and they stood proudly, realizing that they might already have been seen. Forward they went toward a complex of huts quite similar to their own.

Maybe sorrow had restrained the sounds of children playing or females plying their chores. All they heard were the birds. There was no chatter as might be expected of a village, but so many had died that....

The visitants looked around, noting at first a number of ash piles that had once been great burning pyres. The bones of the dead had been carefully taken from them. But no living person was there. Could they be hiding or lying in wait? The women advanced to the center of the village and saw for certain that the settlement had been completely abandoned. Only Morda's huge tusks, coated with volcanic dust, were still there, occupying an erstwhile place of honor. A trail was observable in the layer of ash, making it plain that the entire Noi people had taken flight.

When, after a thorough search, the five women went back to their own village, they triumphantly told what they had discovered. The Noi were gone! What a hubbub followed this announcement! Zan-Gah, who knew the Noi better than most, correctly guessed what had happened. Their tribe, thoroughly unnerved by the great volcanic explosion and terrified as usual by the unfamiliar, had decided that they could not stand against the Ba-Coro. Clearly the magic of their enemies was too powerful! The Ba-Coro lived with wolves and giants. They could double themselves at will. They had unnatural weapons. And now came this tremendous power (who knew from which god?) to back them in battle!

The Noi elders had resigned themselves that they would have to leave this fair country and return to their old desert home. In this perfumed land the gods themselves were allied against them, and it would be useless to continue fighting. In a single day they had gathered their goods and the relics of their dead and quietly left, singing a sorrowful dirge as they trailed through the ashes. The Ba-Coro alone could possess the Beautiful Country.

"I think we might have grown to like each other," Siraka reflected with some sadness.

▼ ▼ ▼

When Dael awakened from his profound and deathlike sleep his family and friends could only gaze. His mother was in shock, almost fainting herself, when she saw his haggard figure standing before her. She held her hand over her mouth in baffled wonderment, unable to move or speak. His overjoyed father hugged his neck and laughed as he caressed the staring, emotionless face. Dael seemed dazed or still residing in the land of death from which he had come. He had fainted many times before, but never for so long. Dael grew dizzy and began to fall again. Thal caught him and Wumna, coming to herself, made haste to put her son on his bed where he fell asleep immediately.

Dael slept peacefully for three days. When he awoke at last, Zan and other friends were there, anxiously tending him. Dael was soon on his feet, but he still seemed absorbed, and even transformed, by the visions he had lately experienced. It could be seen that he was a different person than the truculent warrior he long had been, and was intensely preoccupied with invisible, spiritual matters. Whatever happened to him in his deathlike trance, and as a result of his healing slumber, he now bore himself as one who had discovered on his mystical voyage some basic, elusive, and yet inexorable truth. He clearly understood things that had completely escaped him before; and he knew above all that he had done grievous wrong—to his people, to his friends, even to his enemies, and to his brother.

Everybody expected Dael to resume command of his faction and direct them to hostilities; but he neither showed nor felt the least authority or desire to rule anyone but himself. Everyone looked for the aftermath of rage and violence that often followed his fits. But it did not come, and he surprised his followers by giving no commands of war. He only mysteriously pronounced that the Noi would no longer be their enemies. Did the spirits inform him that the Noi had left the country, or did he only mean to say that he would not fight them again?

A number of people gathered around the recovered warrior. Dael turned to Pax and Rydl, who happened to be standing close together. "I do not remember why I hated you," he said, looking mainly at Pax with dreamy eyes, "only that I did, and that now my heart is free of it; that now I can love you as the dear, dear friends that you have always been."

These words were spoken in soft, unearthly tones, astonishing his hearers as much as his reawakening had. He went on to say that he was sorry for the trouble he had begun and for the blood he had caused to be spilt. As if he had never had a hand in it, Dael pronounced against war and division. Perhaps he had indeed spoken to ancient Aniah in his nether-journey, or even to his lost wife, Lissa-Na, so pacific had he become. One might have thought that a troop of hellish demons had flown away from him, leaving the sick man sane—as though he had long been dreaming sickly things, and being awake was now in his right mind.

What could have wrought this great alteration for the better? In the depths of Dael's knotted and afflicted spirit there had always been much good. Zan knew that! A strand of Dael's innocence, enmeshed in the unruly tangle that was himself, must have remained undisturbed. The worst of us is not entirely bad. Dael's transformation was like his volcano, from which, under intense heat, the snow has melted. It slides away from the mountain, uncovering its true and perfect form. Whatever Dael had undergone either before or after the most recent battle, whatever had occurred within the secret caverns of his soul, he was now chastened and almost physically changed. Purged of all anger and ambition, he was endowed with a new lucidity of mind. And in that clarity he saw that he must leave his people.

"I will no longer live among the Ba-Coro," he said. "I am not fit. Maybe I will return someday to see Zan's coming child, but now I must leave. Oin and Orah, take my pet wolves. I give them to you." He grabbed a leather bag and prepared to depart. Everyone simply stood and watched.

"What do you seek, Dael," Zan asked sorrowfully, "that you would abandon your people for some unfamiliar place?"

"I want to find out where the river goes, Zan-Gah," Dael said with a trace of a smile. Two things were notable about this speech: Dael had always been more interested in the river's source than its destination; and he addressed his twin respectfully by his name of honor, Zan-Gah. The river, Nobla, was far away, but Zan did not dispute, for he knew that his brother spoke of a river different from Nobla or any that foamed. And he knew that his brother would go.

After only a few minutes Dael was ready to depart, a new spear in his hand. His mother Wumna was crying again. To weep was a mother's lot. She had wept when she gave him birth, and often since had joyed or cried over him.

"Must you really go away?" Zan asked. "How can you hope to survive alone in the wilderness?"

"I do have to go, Zan-Gah," he said. "Every night, and even in my last departure to the spirit world, I have seen Hurnoa's face. I have heard her grating, accusing voice, and always she has said the same thing: 'Go, Dael, and leave your people in peace. *Purify yourself!*' Aniah, and Morda, and other spirits said the same thing. There is no choice but to obey. But don't worry, Zan. I will find friends. I intend to visit the crimson people and learn their ways. And perhaps I will not travel alone." Then he amazed everybody again: "Sparrow, will you go along with me?" It had been many days since he had even spoken to her, and now he extended a hand toward her.

That gentle bird was not really surprised by his request. She stood up, for she had been seated, and turned to Rydl, looking into his face for a long moment. Whatever she saw there—or failed to see—she said to Dael as best she could: "Y-y-yes, I will," and took his hand.

"Farewell, my friends. Farewell, Zan-Gah. I love you. I didn't always but I do now." The brothers embraced as they never had since they were laughing little boys wrestling with each other. Zan could not foresee how this once dangerous, malevolent, and murderous man would over many years grow to be an esteemed leader and teacher. He only knew that the demons who had long possessed his twin had departed; that healing and regeneration were still possible, because there is a secret place in every soul that has never yet been wounded.

Artist, teacher, author, and historian **ALLAN RICHARD SHICKMAN** was an art history professor at the University of Northern Iowa for three decades. His first novel, **ZAN-GAH: A PREHISTORIC ADVENTURE**, won an Eric Hoffer Notable Book Award, and was a Finalist for the *ForeWord Magazine* Book of the Year Award. Shickman now lives and writes in St. Louis.